CW00558221

C6
v4

DYING

ARTHUR SCHNITZLER

DYING

Translated from the German by
Anthea Bell

PUSHKIN PRESS
LONDON

After great pain, a formal feeling comes—
The nerves sit ceremonious, like tombs …
Emily Dickinson

English translation © Anthea Bell 2006

First published in German as
Sterben 1895

This edition first published in 2006 by

Pushkin Press
12 Chester Terrace
London NW1 4ND

ISBN (13) 978 1 901285 74 1
ISBN (10) 1 901285 74 X

Cover: *Frau Elsa Kaufmann auf der Gartenbank* 1911
© Lovis Corinth Kunsthalle Kiel

Frontispiece: Arthur Schnitzler
© Roger-Viollet Rex Features

Set in 10 on 12 Baskerville
and printed in Jordan by National Press

DYING

DUSK WAS FALLING, and Marie rose from the bench where she had been sitting for the last half-hour, first reading her book, then looking down the avenue along which Felix would come. He didn't usually keep her waiting. It was a little cooler now, but the air was still mild with the warmth of the May day as it drew to a close.

There were not many people left in the Augarten, and those who had been out walking were making for the gate that would soon be shut. Marie was near the way out of the park herself when she saw Felix. Although he was late, he was walking slowly, and only when his eyes met hers did he quicken his pace slightly. She stopped, waited for him, and as he took the hand she casually offered him and pressed it, smiling, she asked with a note of gentle displeasure in her voice, "Did you have to work all this time?"

He gave her his arm, but did not reply. "Well?" she asked again.

"Yes, dear," he said then, "and I quite forgot to look at the time."

She glanced sideways at him. He seemed paler than usual. "Don't you think," she said lovingly, "it would be better for you to give a little more time to your Marie? Leave your work alone for a while. Then we can walk more together. How about that? Now you'll always be leaving home in my company."

"Well … "

"Yes, indeed, Felix, I'm not leaving you on your own any more." He gave her a swift glance, almost a look of alarm. "What's the matter?" she asked.

"Nothing!"

They had reached the gate of the park, and were out in the lively hurry and bustle of the evening streets. Something of the general subconscious happiness that usually comes with spring seemed to lie over the city. "Well, do you know what we could do?" he asked.

"Now?"

"Go to the Prater."

"Oh no, it's been so cold there recently."

"Come along, it's almost sultry here in the street! We can come straight back again. Let's go!" He spoke in a distracted, abrupt manner.

"Why do you talk like that, Felix?"

"Like what?"

"What is it? You're with me, with your own girl!" But he looked at her with a fixed and absent gaze.

"What is it?" she cried in alarm, holding his arm more firmly.

"Yes, yes," he said, pulling himself together. "Sultry weather, yes, so it is. I'm not being absent-minded—or if I am, you mustn't hold it against me." They set off along the streets to the Prater. Felix was even quieter than usual. The street lamps were already lit.

"Did you go to see Alfred today?" she suddenly asked.

"Why?"

"Well, you said you were going to."

"Did I?"

"You were feeling so tired yesterday evening."

"I was, yes."

"Then you haven't been to see Alfred?"

"No."

"But oh dear, you were still sick yesterday, and now you want to go to the Prater where it's so damp. It really is rash of you."

"Oh, it doesn't matter."

"Don't talk like that. You'll ruin your health."

"Please," he said, in an almost querulous tone, "let's go, let's just go. I'd really like to be in the Prater. We'll visit that place we liked so much before—the garden restaurant, remember? It isn't chilly there."

"Yes, it is!"

"No, really it isn't! And it's very warm today anyway. We can't go home yet, it's too early. And I don't want to eat dinner in town, I don't feel like being inside the walls of some restaurant, and the smoke would be bad for me—I don't want to be in a crowd either, all that noise hurts me." He had spoken fast at first, and louder than usual, but he let his last words die away. Marie clung to his arm more tightly than ever. She was frightened, and said no more because she felt she would sound tearful. His wish for a visit to the quiet restaurant in the Prater, for a spring evening among green foliage and silence, had communicated itself to her. When neither of them had said anything for a while, she saw a slow, weary smile on his lips, and as he turned to her he tried to make that smile a happy one. But knowing him as well as she did, she could easily tell that it was forced.

They were in the Prater now, where the first avenue leading off the main thoroughfare almost disappeared into the dark and led to their destination. There it was, the plain and simple restaurant, its large garden dimly lit, tables not yet laid, chairs leaning up against them. Faint red lights flickered in the globes perched on slender green poles. A few guests were sitting in the garden, with the proprietor himself among them. Marie and Felix walked past, and he rose to greet them, lifting his cap. They opened the door into the garden room, where a few turned-down gaslights were hissing. A youthful waiter had been sitting and dozing in one corner. He quickly rose, made haste to turn the gas up, and then helped the guests off with their coats. They sat down in a dimly lit, comfortable corner, drew their chairs close together, and ordered something to eat and drink without lingering over their choice. Now they were alone except for the dull red light of the lamps blinking at them from the entrance. The far corners of the room were lost in twilight too.

Still they were both silent, until at last the anxious Marie began, in a trembling voice, "Felix, do tell me, what's the matter? I beg you to tell me." And again that smile came to his lips. "Nothing, child," he said, "don't ask. You know my odd moods by now, don't you?"

"Oh yes, I certainly know your moods, but you're not in one of them now. Something has upset you, I can see it has. There must be some reason. Please, Felix, what is it? I beg you, tell me!"

He looked impatient, for the waiter was just bringing

their order. And as she repeated, "Tell me, tell me!" he glanced at the lad and made a gesture of irritation. The waiter withdrew.

"We're alone now," said Marie. She moved closer to him and took both his hands in hers. "What's the matter? What is it? I have to know. Don't you love me any more?" He said nothing. She kissed his hand, which he slowly withdrew from her. "What is it?"

He looked around as if in search of help. "Oh, please, leave me alone, don't ask, don't torment me!"

She let go of his hand and looked him full in the face. "But I want to know."

He rose and took a deep breath, then put both hands to his head and said, "You'll drive me mad! Don't ask!" And he stood there for a while with a fixed gaze, staring into a void. In alarm, she followed his gaze. Then he sat down, breathing more calmly now, and a mild weariness spread over his features. For a few seconds his terrors seemed to have left him, and he said quietly and affectionately to Marie, "Do eat something, have something to drink."

She obediently picked up knife and fork and asked, but still with alarm in her voice, "What about you?"

"Yes, yes," he replied, but he went on sitting there motionless and touched nothing.

"Then I can't eat anything either," she said, and at that he did begin to eat and drink, but soon he silently laid down his knife and fork, leaned his head on his hand, and looked away from Marie. She watched him for a little while with her lips compressed, then removed the arm that was hiding his face from her. Now she saw the brightness in his eyes, and just as she cried out, "Oh, Felix, Felix!" he began to sob and weep hot tears. She laid his head against her breast, stroked his hair, kissed his forehead, tried to kiss away his tears. "Felix, Felix!" And his weeping grew quieter and quieter. "What is it, darling, my only beloved dear one, do tell me!"

Then, with his head still against her breast so that his words came to her with a heavy, hollow sound, he said, "Marie, Marie, I didn't want to tell you. One more year and then it will all be over." Now he was weeping violently and loudly.

She sat there as pale as death, eyes wide open, not understanding, not wanting to understand. Something cold and terrible constricted her throat, until she suddenly cried out, "Felix, Felix," flung herself in front of him and looked into the tearful, desperate face that had now sunk to his chest. He saw her kneeling before him and whispered, "Get up, get up!" She did so, mechanically obeying his words, and sat down opposite him. She couldn't speak, she couldn't ask any questions. And he, after a few seconds of deep silence, suddenly cried out, wailing aloud with his eyes raised as if something incomprehensible was weighing down on him "It's terrible! Terrible!"

She recovered her voice. "Come, come! … " But she could say no more.

"Yes, let's go," he said, making a movement as if to shake something off. He called to the waiter, paid, and they quickly left the restaurant together.

Outside, the spring night surrounded them in silence. Marie stopped in the dark avenue and took her lover's hand. "Now, tell me about it."

He was perfectly calm now, and what he told her sounded as plain and simple as if it were really a minor matter. He freed his hand and stroked her face. It was so dark that they could barely see each other.

"You mustn't be frightened, sweetheart, a year is a long, long time. You understand, that's it: I have only a year to live."

She cried out, "Oh no, you're crazy, you're crazy!"

"It's pitiful of me to tell you at all, and stupid too. But you see, being the only one to know, going about feeling so lonely, always with that thought in my mind—I really couldn't have endured it for long. And perhaps it's a good thing for you to get used to it. But come along, why are we standing here? I'm used to the idea now myself, Marie. It's been a long time since I believed anything Alfred said."

"So you didn't go to see Alfred? But other doctors don't know anything."

"You see, child, I've suffered so much from the uncertainty these last few weeks. It's better now. Now at least I know. I went to see Professor Bernard and at least he told me the truth."

"No, no, he didn't. I'm sure he just wanted to frighten you to make you take more care of yourself."

"My dear child, I've had a very serious conversation with the man. I had to know for sure. For your sake too."

"Felix, Felix," she cried, flinging both arms around him. "What are you saying? I won't live a day without you, not an hour."

"Come, come," he said quietly. "Calm down." They had reached the way out of the Prater. The scene around them was lively now, bright and noisy. Carriages rattling along the roads, trams whistling and ringing their bells, the heavy rumble of a railway train passing over the bridge above them. Marie shivered. All this liveliness suddenly had something scornful and hostile about it, and it hurt her. She led him the way she wanted to go, avoiding the broad main thoroughfare and making their way home along quiet side streets instead.

For a moment it occurred to her that he ought to take a cab, but she hesitated to say so. They could always walk slowly.

"You're not going to die, no, no," she said under her breath, leaning her head against his shoulder. "I can't live without you."

"My dear child, you'll change your mind. I've thought it all out carefully. Indeed I have. Do you know, when the line was suddenly drawn like that, I saw it all so distinctly, so clearly."

"No line's been drawn."

"I know it's hard to believe, darling. At this moment I don't believe it myself. It's so hard to grasp, isn't it? Just think, here I am walking along beside you, speaking words out loud, words that you can hear, and in a year I'll be lying cold in the ground, perhaps already rotting away."

"Stop it, stop it!"

"And you'll look as you do now. Just as you look now, perhaps still a little pale from weeping, but then another evening will come, and many more, and summer and autumn and winter, and another spring—and then I'll have been dead and cold for a year—what's the matter?"

She was weeping bitterly. Her tears ran over her cheeks and down her throat.

A despairing smile passed over his face, and he whispered through his teeth, hoarsely, harshly, "I'm sorry."

She was still sobbing as they walked on, and he said no more. Their way led past the Stadtpark, along dark, quiet, broad streets with a faint, sad scent of lilac wafting over them from the shrubs in the park. They slowly went on their way. Tall grey and yellow buildings, all much the same, stood on the other side of the street. The mighty dome of the Karlskirche towering into the blue night sky was closer now. They turned down a side street, and had soon reached the building where they lived. Slowly, they climbed the dimly lit stairs, and heard servant girls gossiping and giggling behind the corridor windows and doors. After a few minutes they had closed their own door behind them. The window was open; the air was perfumed by the scent of a few dark roses standing in a plain vase on the bedside table. A faint humming sound rose from the street outside. They both went to the window. All was dark and still in the building opposite. Then he sat down on the sofa, she closed the shutters and drew the curtains, lit a candle and put it on the table. He had not been watching any of this, but sat deep in thought. She came close to him. "Felix!" she cried.

He looked up and smiled. "Well, child?" he asked. Gently as he spoke, in a soft, quiet voice, a sense of infinite fear overwhelmed her. Oh, she didn't want to lose him. Never! Never, never! It wasn't true. It simply was not possible. She tried to say something, to tell him all this, but when she threw herself down on the floor in front of him she couldn't find the strength to speak. She laid her head on his knees and wept. His hands rested on her hair.

"Don't cry," he whispered tenderly. "Not any more, sweetheart."

She raised her head, clutching at a wonderful hope. "It isn't true, is it? Surely it isn't true?"

He kissed her lips, long and ardently. Then he said almost harshly, "Yes, it's true," rose, went to the window and stood in the shadows there. The flickering candle-light played only on the floor at his feet. After a while he began talking again. "You'll have to get used to the idea. Just think we're parting like *this*. You don't have to tell yourself I'm not in this world any more."

She didn't seem to be listening, and had hidden her face in the sofa cushions. He went on. "Think about it philo-sophically, and then it's not so terrible. After all, we still have so much time to be happy, don't we, sweetheart?"

She suddenly looked at him from great, tearless eyes. Then she hurried over, clung to him, held him close to her breast with both arms. "I want to die with you" she whispered.

He smiled. "That's childish. I'm not as small-minded as you think me. And I have no right at all to take you with me."

"I can't live without you."

"But think how long you lived without me before! I was already doomed when I met you a year ago. I didn't know it, but even then I had a presentiment."

"You don't know now."

"Yes, I do. That's why I want you to have your freedom, beginning today." She clung all the closer. "Take it, take it," he said. She did not reply, but looked up at him as if she didn't understand.

"You're so beautiful, and ah! so healthy. You have every right to life. Leave me alone."

She cried out. "I've lived with you, I'll die with you."

He kissed her brow. "You won't, I forbid it. You must put that idea out of your head."

"I swear—"

"Don't swear anything. One day you'd be asking me to release you from your word."

"So that's what you think of me!"

"Oh, I know you love me. You won't leave me until—"

"I'll never, never leave you." He shook his head. She nestled close to him, took both his hands and kissed them.

"You're so good," he said. "It makes me very sad."

"Don't be sad. Whatever happens we'll share the same fate."

"No," he said firmly and gravely, "don't say that. I'm not like other people. I don't want to be like them. I understand it all, but it would be pitiful of me to listen to you any longer, to let you intoxicate me with what you say in the first moment of pain. I must go and you must stay."

She had begun weeping again. He caressed and kissed her to calm her down, and they stayed there by the window, no longer talking. The minutes passed, the candle burned lower.

After some time Felix moved away from her and sat down on the sofa. He felt a heavy weariness. Marie went to sit beside him, gently took his head in her hands and moved it to her shoulder. He looked at her lovingly and closed his eyes, and so he fell asleep.

Morning came, pale and cool. Felix woke up. His head was still on her breast, but she was sleeping a sound, deep sleep. He moved quietly away from her and went to the window, looked down at the street where it lay deserted in the first light of dawn. He shivered. After a few moments he stretched out on the bed, fully clothed, and stared up at the ceiling.

It was full daylight when he woke again. Marie was sitting on the edge of the bed and had kissed him awake. They both smiled. Had it all been just a bad dream? He himself felt so healthy and refreshed now. And the sun was laughing outside. Sounds came up from the street; it was all so full of life. A number of windows were open in the building opposite, and breakfast was on the table, the same as every morning. The room was bright; daylight filled every corner. Motes of dust danced in the sunbeams, and everywhere, everywhere there was hope, hope, hope!

The doctor was smoking his afternoon cigar when a lady was announced. Alfred's consulting hours had not begun yet, and he was rather displeased. "Marie" he cried in surprise as she came in.

"Please don't be cross with me for disturbing you so early. Oh, do go on smoking."

"Well, if I may. But what is it? What's the matter?"

She stood before him, one hand on his desk, the other holding her sunshade. "Is it true?" She uttered the words hastily. "Is it really true that Felix is so ill? Oh, you look pale. Why didn't you tell me, why not?"

"What can you be thinking of?" He strode up and down the room. "This is foolish conduct. Please sit down."

"Answer me."

"He's certainly unwell. That can't be news to you."

"He's doomed," she cried.

"Come, come!"

"I know he is; *he* knows too. He went to see Professor Bernard yesterday, and the Professor told him."

"Many a professor has been mistaken."

"You've often examined him. Tell me the truth."

"There's no absolute truth in such cases."

"I see—you don't want to say it because he's your friend, isn't that so? Yes, I can tell from your face. So it's true, it's true. Oh God, oh God!"

"My dear child, do calm down."

She looked quickly up at him. "*Is* it true?"

"Well, he's ill, you know he is."

"Ah—"

"But why did the Professor tell him? And then—"

"Then? Then? Oh, please don't give me hope if there isn't any."

"These things can never be predicted for certain. It could take a long time yet."

"I know how long. A year."

Alfred compressed his lips. "Can you tell me why he consulted another doctor?"

"Oh, because he knew you'd never tell him the truth—that's all."

"This is stupid," the doctor said in annoyance, "just stupid. I can't make it out! As if it were so urgently necessary to tell a man—"

At this moment the door opened and Felix came in.

"I thought as much," he said, on seeing Marie.

"Nice tricks you get up to!" cried the doctor. "Nice tricks, I must say."

"You can forget your fine phrases, my dear Alfred" replied Felix. "I'm very grateful for your goodwill—you've been a good friend, you've been wonderful."

Here Marie interrupted. "He says the Professor can't be cer—"

"Never mind that," Felix interrupted. "You've all been able to keep me deluding myself up to this point. Taking it any further now would be a tasteless joke."

"You're little more than a child," said Alfred. "There are many people walking around Vienna today who were told, twenty years ago, that they were on the point of death."

"But most such people really are dead and buried."

Alfred paced up and down the room. "Once and for

all, nothing's changed between yesterday and today. You'll look after yourself more carefully now, that's all, you'll be following my advice better, which is all to the good. Only a week ago I was examining a man of fifty who—"

"Yes, I know," Felix interrupted. "A man of fifty who was given up as a hopeless case at the age of twenty, and now he's the picture of health and has eight healthy children."

"Such things do happen, you can't deny it," objected Alfred.

"The fact is," replied Felix, "I'm not the kind of man to attract miracles."

"Miracles?" exclaimed Alfred. "I'm talking about perfectly natural phenomena."

"But look at him, do," said Marie. "I think he looks better now than he did last winter."

"He just has to be careful of himself" repeated Alfred, stopping in front of his friend. "You two had better go for a stay in the mountains now and take things easy. Really easy."

"Oh yes, when shall we start?" asked Marie eagerly.

"This is all nonsense," said Felix.

"And then in the autumn you should go south."

"And what about next spring?" enquired Felix ironically.

"Let's hope you're better then," cried Marie.

"Better, yes," laughed Felix. "Better! Well, at least my sufferings will be over."

"I always say," remarked the doctor "none of these great clinicians know the first thing about psychology."

"Because they don't realise that we can't bear the truth" pointed out Felix.

"There are no hard and fast truths, I tell you. That man thought he'd better put the fear of God into you to keep you from doing anything reckless. That, roughly speaking, will have been the way his mind worked. And then, if you do get better in spite of his predictions, he doesn't lose face because he was only warning you."

"Let's stop this childish argument" Felix said here. "I had a very serious conversation with the man, I made it very clear to him that I have to know for certain. Family matters, I said! That always impresses people. And to be honest with you, I'll admit that the uncertainty was too hard to bear."

"It's not as if you were certain now," Alfred objected.

"Yes, I am certain now. You're going to unnecessary trouble. All I have to think of at this point is how to spend my last year as wisely as possible. Wait and see, my dear Alfred, I'm a man who will leave this world smiling. No, don't cry, sweetheart; you've no idea how delightful you'll still find the world without me. Don't you agree, Alfred?"

"Oh, for goodness' sake, you're distressing the girl unnecessarily."

"It's true, a complete break would be more sensible. Please leave me, sweetheart, let me die alone!"

"Give me some poison!" Marie suddenly demanded of the doctor.

"You're both out of your minds," cried Alfred.

"Poison! I don't want to live a second longer than he

does, and I want him to believe it. But he won't. Why not? Why not?"

"Listen, sweetheart, I have something to say to you now. If you mention such nonsense once again, just *once* again, I shall disappear without trace. Then you won't see me again anyway. I have no right to chain your fate to mine, and I don't want the responsibility."

"And you listen to me, my dear Felix," began the doctor. "You will kindly be good enough to leave the city today rather than tomorrow. You can't go on like this. I shall take the pair of you to the railway station this evening, and I hope peace and quiet and good invigorating air will help you both to see reason again."

"I entirely agree with you" said Felix. "It makes no difference to me where—"

"And moreover," Alfred interrupted "there's no reason at all to despair for the moment, so you can stop making dismal remarks."

"A great psychologist!" said Felix, smiling. "When a doctor's so rough with his patient, the patient feels better at once."

"More than anything else I'm your friend. So as you know, you should—"

"Leave—tomorrow—for the mountains!"

"Yes, quite so."

"Well, thank you very much, anyway," said Felix, shaking hands with his friend. "And now we'll be off. I can hear someone clearing his throat outside already. Come along, sweetheart!"

"Thank you, Doctor," said Marie as they left.

"No need to thank me. Just be a sensible girl and look after him. Goodbye, then."

On the steps outside, Felix said abruptly, "A nice fellow, the Doctor, don't you think?"

"Oh, yes."

"And young and healthy, with perhaps another forty years in front of him—or a hundred."

They were out in the street now, surrounded by people who were talking and walking, laughing and living, without a thought of death in their minds.

They found a small house close to the lake. It stood a little way from the village itself, one of the last stragglers in the row of houses beside the water. Behind the house, meadows covered the hills, and further up there were fields full of summer flowers. Far beyond those, only occasionally visible, was the indistinct outline of the distant mountain range. And when they came out of their house on to the balcony that stood on four damp brown stilts above the clear water, they were looking straight at a long line of rocks on the opposite bank of the lake, with the cold gleam of the silent sky resting above them.

During the first days of their stay here, they had felt wonderfully peaceful in a way that they themselves could hardly understand. It was as if the general fate of all mankind had power over them only where they usually lived; here, in these new surroundings, the sentence of death pronounced in another world no longer held good. Not since they first met had they found solitude so refreshing. Sometimes they would look at one another as if there had been some small incident in the immediate past, maybe a quarrel or a misunderstanding, but it mustn't be mentioned again. On those fine summer days Felix felt so well that soon after his arrival he said he wanted to get back to work. Marie didn't agree. "You're not entirely better yet," she smiled. And the sunlight danced on the little table where Felix had stacked his books and papers, while soft, caressing air that knew nothing of all the world's unhappiness wafted in from the lake and through the window.

One evening, as their habit was, they hired an old man from the village to row them out on the lake. The boat was a good, sturdy craft with an upholstered seat where Marie would sit while Felix lay at her feet, wrapped in a warm grey rug that served as both cushion and blanket. He had laid his head on her knees. A light mist lay over the placid, broad expanse of water, and it seemed as if twilight were slowly rising from the lake and spreading gradually to the banks. Today Felix ventured to smoke a cigar, and he looked out over the rippling lake to the rocks with their summits bathed in muted yellow sunlight.

"Tell me, sweetheart" he began, "do you dare to look up?"

"Look up where?"

He pointed to the sky. "Right up there, into the dark blue. I can't do it myself. It strikes me as eerie."

She looked up, letting her glance rest on the sky for some seconds. "I rather like it," she said.

"You do? When the sky's as clear as it is today, I can't

make sense of it at all. That distance, that terrible distance! If there are clouds up there I don't feel so ill at ease, the clouds are part of our world—I'm looking at something I know."

"There'll most likely be rain tomorrow," remarked the boatman. "The mountains look too close today!" And he let the oars rest so that the boat glided over the water in silence more and more slowly.

Felix cleared his throat. "How odd; I'm not really enjoying this cigar."

"Throw it away, then!"

Felix turned the glowing cigar in his fingers once or twice, then threw it into the water, and said, without turning to Marie "Well, I suppose I'm not quite better yet."

"Oh, hush!" she contradicted him, caressing his hair gently with her hand.

"What are we going to do if it rains?" asked Felix. "You'll have to let me work then."

"No, you mustn't."

She leaned down and looked into his eyes. It struck her that his cheeks were flushed. "I'll soon drive away your gloomy thoughts! Don't you think it's time to go home? It's turning chilly now."

"Chilly? I don't feel cold."

"Oh, well, you have your thick rug."

"What an egotist I am!" he cried. "I quite forgot you were wearing a summer dress." He turned to the boatman. "Home, please." A few hundred oar-strokes, and they were close to their house. Then Marie noticed that

Felix was clasping his left wrist in his right hand. "What is it?" she asked.

"Sweetheart, it's true, I'm not quite better yet."

"But … "

"I must be feverish. How stupid!"

"I'm sure you're wrong," said Marie anxiously. "But I'll go for the doctor at once."

"Oh, for goodness' sake, that's all I need!"

They had come to the bank and went ashore. It was almost dark indoors, but their rooms still held the day's warmth. While Marie prepared their evening meal Felix sat quietly in an armchair.

"Do you realise?" he said suddenly. "Our first week here is over."

She came quickly over from setting the table and put both arms round him. "What is it?"

He freed himself. "Ah, never mind that!" Rising, he sat down at the table, and she followed. He drummed his fingers on the table-top. "I feel so defenceless. It suddenly comes over one."

"Oh, Felix, Felix." She drew her chair close to his. He was looking around the room, eyes very wide. Then he shook his head with annoyance, as if irritated by something that he couldn't grasp, and said between his teeth, "Defenceless! I'm defenceless! No one can help me. The thing itself isn't so terrible—but it's being so defence-less!"

"Felix, please, don't agitate yourself. I'm sure it's nothing. But would you like me … just to reassure you … would you like me to go for the doctor?"

"Oh please, stop that! I'm really sorry to keep entertaining you with talk of my illness."

"But——"

"It won't happen again. Pour me some more wine, will you? Yes, yes, some more—thank you. Now, talk to me about something."

"About what?"

"Anything. Read aloud if you can't think of anything to say. Oh, I'm sorry, after supper, of course. Eat your supper, and I'll eat too." He picked up knife and fork. "I even have an appetite. This tastes really good."

"There we are, then," said Marie, forcing a smile. And they both ate and drank.

The next few days brought warm rain, and they sat sometimes indoors, sometimes out on the balcony until evening. They both read, or looked out of the window, or he watched her when she picked up a piece of needlework. Now and then they played cards, and he taught her the rudiments of chess. At other times he lay on the sofa, and she sat beside him to read aloud. Those were quiet days and evenings, and Felix really did feel quite well. He was glad to discover that the bad weather didn't affect him, and his fever did not return.

One afternoon, when the sky seemed to be clearing at last after a long rainy period, they were sitting on the balcony again, and Felix said abruptly, without referring back to any earlier conversation:

"In fact the whole world is full of people condemned to death."

Marie looked up from her needlework.

"For instance" he went on, "suppose someone told you: young lady, you're going to die on the first of May 1970. You'd spend the whole of the rest of your life in nameless dread of the first of May 1970, although I feel sure you don't at this moment seriously believe you'll live to be a hundred."

She did not reply.

He went on, looking out at the lake, which was just beginning to gleam as the sunlight broke through. "Other people are walking around now, confident and healthy, but some stupid accident will carry them off within a few weeks. They aren't thinking of death at all, are they?"

"Oh dear," said Marie "stop thinking such stupid things, do! Surely even you realise that you're getting better."

He smiled.

"I mean, you of all people are one of the kind who do get better."

That made him laugh out loud. "My dear child, do you seriously think Fate can take me in? Do you think I'm deceived by this apparent sense of well-being, Nature's gift to me just now? It's purely by chance that I know how things are with me, and the thought of imminent death makes me a philosopher—like other great men in their time."

"Stop it at once, will you?"

"Oho, my dear young lady, so I'm to die and you're

not even to suffer the minor inconvenience of hearing me talk about it?"

She threw aside her needlework and went over to him. "I can feel," she said in a tone of genuine conviction, "I can feel that you'll stay with me. You can't be the judge of your own recovery. What you have to do now is stop thinking about it, and then this dark shadow will lift from our lives."

He looked at her for a long time. "You really do seem absolutely unable to grasp it. I must make it more obvious. Look at this." He picked up a newspaper. "What does it say?"

"The twelfth of June 1890."

"That's right, 1890. Now imagine the number at the end of that date is one instead of zero. When the date says that, it will all be over. Now do you understand?"

She snatched the newspaper from him and threw it angrily on the floor.

"It's not the paper's fault," he said calmly. And suddenly, rising energetically and apparently making a swift decisions to dismiss all such thoughts, he cried, "Look, how beautiful! See the sun over the water—and there," he added, leaning over the balcony and looking at the low-lying land on the other side "see the crops in the fields moving in the wind. I'd like to go out for a little while."

"Won't it be too damp for you?"

"Come along, I need some fresh air."

She dared not oppose him.

They both took their hats, put on their coats, and set off along the path leading to the fields. The sky was almost completely clear now. White mist drifted over the distant outline of the mountains, forming a multitude of different shapes. The green of the meadows was almost lost in the white-gold radiance that seemed to surround the whole area. Soon the path brought them to the middle of the cornfields, and they had to walk in single file while blades rustled as they brushed the hems of their coats. Before long they turned off the track into a wood of broad-leaved trees, not too dense, with well-tended pathways and benches at frequent intervals where walkers could sit down and rest. Here they went arm-in-arm.

"Isn't this beautiful?" cried Felix. "And the air's so fragrant!"

"Don't you think that now, after the rain—" Marie objected, but she left her sentence unfinished.

He shook his head impatiently. "Never mind that, what does the rain have to do with it? I don't like being given warnings all the time."

As they walked on, the wood thinned out more and more. The lake, barely a hundred paces away now, glinted through the leaves. Where the wood petered out with a few sparse bushes, a narrow tongue of land extended into the water. A few spruce-wood benches and tables stood here, and there was a wooden fence beside the bank. A slight evening breeze had risen and was driving waves to the shore. And now the wind blew further on, through the bushes and above the trees, making water drip off the wet leaves again. The faint light of day as it drew to its close lay over the water.

"I never guessed" said Felix, "how beautiful all this is."

"It's lovely, yes."

"But you don't know!" cried Felix. "You can't know, you don't have to go away and leave it." And he slowly took a few steps forward and leaned both arms on the slight structure of the fence. The water washed around its narrow posts, and he looked out over the shimmering lake for a long time. Then he turned. Marie was standing behind him, her eyes sad with the tears she was holding back.

"You see," said Felix jokingly "I'm leaving you all this as a legacy. Yes, I am indeed, for it belongs to me. That's the secret of being alive, and I've discovered it: it's the sense you have of owning everything. I could do what I liked with all these things. I could make flowers grow on the bare rock over there, I could drive the white clouds out of the sky. I don't do it because it's beautiful just the way it is. My dear child, only when you're alone will you understand me. Yes, then you'll feel that all this has passed into your possession."

He took her hand and drew her close to him. Then he gestured with his other arm as though to show her all the beauty of the scene. "All this, all this," he said. But since she still remained silent, and her eyes were as wide and dry as ever, he broke off abruptly and said "Well, let's go home!"

Dusk was falling, and they took the path along the bank, which soon brought them back to their lodgings. "It was a delightful walk" said Felix.

She silently nodded.

"We must take it more often, sweetheart."

"Yes," she said.

"And" he added, in a tone of derisive pity, "and I won't torment you either, no, never."

One afternoon soon after this he decided to start work again. As he was about to put pencil to paper for the first time, he glanced at Marie with a certain mischievous curiosity, to see if she would try to stop him. But she said nothing. Soon he put his paper and pencil aside and picked up the first book that came to hand. Reading it was a better way to occupy his mind. He wasn't capable of working yet. He would have to reach the point where he entirely despised life, and was looking forward with composure to silent eternity, before he could write his last will and testament, which was to be like the words of a sage. So he planned it. Not a last will and testament of the kind written by ordinary people, a document that always betrays their secret fear of death. Nor was this work to deal with anything that could be grasped and seen but must fall into ruin at last, some time after he did: *his* testament was to be a poem, a quiet, smiling farewell to the world over which he had triumphed. He said nothing to Marie about these thoughts. She wouldn't have understood him. He felt that he and she were so different. With a certain pride in himself, he sat opposite her during the long afternoons when, as so often, she had fallen asleep over her book, her loose hair curling on her forehead. His self-awareness grew as he saw how much he could hide from her. He was becoming so isolated, so great.

That afternoon, as her eyelids closed again, he quietly slipped out of the house. He went walking in the wood, surrounded by the silence of the sultry summer afternoon. And now he realised that it could happen today. He breathed deeply, he felt so light, so free. He went on under the heavy shade of the trees. The muted daylight flowed pleasurably over him. He felt it was all a stroke of good fortune: the shade, the peace, the soft air. He drank it in. There was no pain in the thought that he was to lose this life with all its tenderness. "Lose it, lose it," he said in an undertone to himself. He took a deep breath, and drew the air into his lungs so easily and deliciously that he suddenly couldn't grasp the fact that he was ill at all. But he *was* ill, he was doomed. And all at once a kind of enlightenment came to him, and he realised that he didn't believe it. That was a fact, that was why he felt so free and so well, and that was why it seemed to him that today the right time had come. He had not overcome his love of life, but his fear of death had left him because he didn't believe in death any more. He knew he was one of those who would be cured, and felt as if something sleeping had woken to new life in a hidden corner of his soul. He felt impelled to open his eyes further, take greater strides forward, breathe yet more deeply. The day grew lighter, life more vivid. So that was it, that was it! And why? Why did he suddenly feel so intoxicated by hope again? Ah, hope! It was more than that. It was certainty. Even this morning his thoughts had still tormented him, had clutched at his throat—and now, now he was better, better. He cried it out loud. "I'm better!"

Here he reached the end of the wood. Before him lay the lake, deep-blue and gleaming. He dropped on a bench and sat there in deep content, looking at the water. He thought how strange it was that the joy of his recovery had disguised itself as the desire to take a proud farewell of the world.

There was a slight sound behind him. He hardly had time to turn round. It was Marie. Her eyelids were fluttering, her face was slightly flushed.

"What's the matter?"

"Why did you go out? Why did you leave me alone? I was so frightened."

"Oh, come on," he said, pulling her down to sit beside him. He smiled and kissed her. She had such warm, full lips. "Come here," he said quietly, taking her on his lap. She nestled close to him, putting her arms round his neck. And she was beautiful! A sultry perfume rose from her blonde hair, and endless love rose in him for this supple, fragrant being against his breast. Tears came to his eyes, and he took her hands to kiss them. He loved her so much!

From the lake came a faint buzzing sound. They both looked up, rose, and went closer to the bank, arm-in-arm. The steamer was in sight in the distance. They waited until it was close enough for them to make out the figures of passengers on deck, and then turned away and strolled home through the wood. They walked arm-in-arm and slowly, smiling at one another now and then, and speaking again the words they had spoken in their first days of love. Sweet questions passed between them, tentatively affectionate, and ardent words of cajolery and assurance. And they were cheerful, they were children once again, and happy.

Oppressive, sweltering summer weather had come with hot, burning days and mild lascivious nights. Every day was like the day before, every night like the night just past; time stood still. And they were on their own. They thought of nothing but each other, the wood, the lake, the little house—that was their world. Pleasant sultry air surrounded them, and in it they forgot to think. Carefree, laughing nights and weary but tender days flowed by.

It was on one of those nights, when the candle was still burning late, that Marie, who had been lying with her eyes open, sat up in bed. She looked at her lover's face, full of the peace of deep sleep. She listened to his breathing. It was as good as certain now: every hour was bringing him closer to a cure. Unutterable depths of emotion filled her, and she leaned close to him to feel his breath on her cheeks. How beautiful life was! And he, he alone, was her whole life. Ah, she had him back now, she had him back again, back again for ever!

The sleeping man drew a breath that sounded different from his breathing until now, and it disturbed her. A soft, stifled moan. A look of suffering had appeared on his lips as they opened slightly, and with alarm she saw drops of sweat on his forehead. He had turned his head a little way aside. But then his lips closed again.

The peaceful expression returned to his face, and after a moment's uneasiness his breathing too became regular again, almost silent. But Marie was suddenly in the grip of a fear that tormented her. She would have liked to wake him, nestle close to him, feel his warmth, his life, his very being. A strange pang of guilt assailed her, and all at once her happy belief that he would be saved seemed to her like tempting Providence. She tried persuading herself that it hadn't been a firm belief, oh no, just a quiet, thankful hope, and she needn't be too cruelly punished for that. She swore to herself not to be so thoughtlessly happy again. All at once those times when she was dizzy with joy became times of thoughtless sinfulness for which she must atone. Of course! And then, wasn't what others thought of as sin quite different for them? A love that could perhaps work wonders? Might not these last few sweet nights be the very thing that would restore him to health?

A dreadful groan issued from Felix's mouth. He had sat up in bed in alarm, half-asleep, eyes wide and staring into space in a way that made Marie cry out. That woke him fully. "What is it, what is it?" he said. Marie could find no words. "Did you cry out, Marie? I heard someone cry out." He was breathing very fast. "I felt I was choking. I had a dream too, but I can't remember it."

"I was so startled," she stammered.

"And I feel cold now, Marie."

"Well, yes," she said, "you're having bad dreams."

"Oh, what of it?" And he looked up angrily. "I'm feverish again, that's what it is." His teeth were chattering; he lay down and pulled the covers over him.

She looked around desperately. "Shall I—would you like—"

"I wouldn't like anything. Just go to sleep! I'm tired, I'll get some sleep too. Leave the light on." He closed his eyes and pulled the covers over his mouth. Marie dared not ask him any more questions. She knew how much sympathy embittered him when he wasn't well. He fell asleep after a few minutes, but she couldn't sleep any more. Soon grey streaks of dawn light began creeping into the room. These first, muted signs of the coming morning did Marie good. She felt as if something smiling and friendly were coming to visit them, and had a strange urge to go out to greet the morning. Very quietly she got out of bed, quickly wrapped her house-dress around her, and crept out on the terrace. The sky, the mountains, the lake were still all blurred in dark, uncertain grey. It was strangely pleasurable to strain her eyes a little to discern outlines more clearly. She sat in the armchair and let her eyes gaze into the twilight. Unutterable contentment flowed through Marie as she leaned back in the deep silence of the summer dawn. Around her, everything was so peaceful, so mild, so eternal. It was so lovely to be alone for a while like this, amidst the great silence—and away from the cramped, stuffy room. A realisation suddenly came to her: she had been glad to rise and leave his side, she was glad to be here, glad to be alone!

All day thoughts of the night just past came back to her. They were not as tormenting, as sinister as they had been in the darkness, but they were all the clearer for that, and they had a bearing on her decisions. Above all, she decided that as far as possible she must moderate the vehemence of his love. She couldn't understand why she hadn't thought of that before. But now she would go about it so gently and tactfully that it wouldn't seem like rejection, only a new and better kind of love.

However, she did not need to be particularly tactful and gentle. His stormy passion seemed to have died down since that night; he himself treated Marie with a weary affection that at first soothed her and ultimately struck her as strange. He read a great deal during the day, or merely seemed to be reading, for often she noticed him looking up from his book and into space. Their conversation touched on a thousand everyday things, and nothing of importance, but without making Marie feel that he was no longer admitting her to his secret thoughts. It all happened quite naturally, as if all those undertones of indifference in him were only a convalescent's cheerful languor. He lay in bed late in the morning, while she had adopted the habit of going out-of-doors at first light. Then she either sat on the balcony or went down to the lake and, without moving from the bank, sat in a boat and let the gently moving water rock her. Now and then she went walking in the wood, so when she entered the bedroom to wake him she was usually coming back from a little morning outing. She was glad of his healthy sleep, which she saw as a good sign. She didn't know how often he woke in the night, and she didn't see the glance of endless grief that rested on her while she herself lay deep in the healthy sleep of youth.

Once, when she had climbed into the boat in the morning and the early sun was sprinkling the lake with its first golden sparks of light, she was overcome by a wish to venture further out on the shining clear water. She rowed some way, and as she was not very good at it she exerted herself a great deal, which increased her enjoyment of the boat ride. Even as early as this you were never entirely alone on the water. Several boats met Marie, and she thought some of them came closer to her on purpose. One small, elegant craft rowed by two young men passed her very fast at close quarters. The gentlemen pulled in their oars, raised their caps, and wished her good morning with civil smiles.

Marie stared at the two of them, and unthinkingly said "Good morning" herself. Then she watched the young men move away, hardly aware of what she was doing. They themselves had turned to wave once more. Suddenly it entered her mind that she had done something wrong, and she rowed back as quickly as her modest skill allowed. It took her almost half an hour to get to shore, and she arrived heated and with her hair untidy. From the water she had seen Felix sitting on the balcony, and now she quickly went into the house. In confusion, as if conscious of some guilty act, she hurried to the balcony, put her arms around Felix from behind, and asked jokingly, in exaggerated high spirits, "Guess who?"

He slowly withdrew from her embrace and looked

askance at her. "What is it? What makes you so cheerful?"

"Being back with you."

"Why are you so hot? You're glowing!"

"Oh goodness! I'm happy, so happy, so happy!" In high spirits, she pushed the rug off his knees and sat on his lap. She felt annoyed first with her own awkwardness, then with his sullen face, and kissed him on the lips.

"And what makes you so happy?"

"Don't I have good reason? I'm so glad that ... " Here she hesitated and then went on. "That it's been lifted from you.'

"What has?" There was something like distrust in his question.

She had to go on now, there was nothing for it. "Well, the fear."

"The fear of death, you mean?"

"Don't say it out loud."

"Why do you say it's been lifted from *me*? From you too, surely?" So saying he looked at her searchingly and almost with ill-will. And when, instead of answering, she ruffled his hair with her hands and brought her mouth close to his brow, he leaned his head back slightly and went on, cold and relentless, "At least—wasn't that what you once wanted? My fate was to be yours too, wasn't it?"

"And so it will be," she cried in a vivacious, cheerful voice.

"No, it will not," he gravely interrupted her. "Why are we glossing it over? 'It' has not been taken from me. 'It' is coming closer, I feel that."

"But ... " Imperceptibly, she had moved away from him, and was now leaning on the balcony rail. He got to his feet and walked up and down.

"Yes, I can feel it. It's my duty to tell you, anyway. If it happened suddenly, you would probably be too violently alarmed. So I will remind you that almost a quarter of the time left to me is gone. Or perhaps I'm only persuading myself that I must tell you—and nothing but cowardice makes me do it."

"Are you angry," she said apprehensively, "because I left you alone?"

"Nonsense!" he was quick to reply. "If I could see you cheerful, then if I know my own nature I myself would wait for the day that's coming cheerfully enough,. But your merriment, to be honest, is something I find hard to bear. So I'm leaving you free to separate your life from mine within the next few days."

"Felix!" He was still pacing up and down, and she held him back with both arms. He shook free again.

"The worst time is coming. Until now I've been an interesting invalid. Slightly pale, coughing a little, slightly melancholy. A woman can quite like that. But my child, you should spare yourself what lies ahead now. It could poison your memory of me."

She sought in vain for an answer, and stared at him helplessly.

"You think that's difficult to accept? There'd be no love in it at the end, it could even be terrible. I'm telling you that now so there can be no doubt about it. Indeed you'll be doing me and my vanity a great service by accepting my suggestion. For at least I want you to think of the past with pain, to shed real tears for me. What I don't want is to have you sitting by my bed day and night thinking: if only it were over, since it has to be over some time—and feeling a sense of release when I do leave you."

She struggled to find words. At last she managed to say, "I'll stay with you for ever."

He ignored that. "We won't talk about it any more. In a week's time, I think, I'll go back to Vienna. I have much to put in order. Before we leave this house I'll ask you my question—no, put my request to you again."

"Felix! I—"

He interrupted her violently. "I won't have you saying another word on the subject until then, and I'll decide on the time myself." Leaving the balcony, he turned to the bedroom. She was about to follow him. "Leave me now," he said gently. "I want to be alone for a little while."

She stayed on the balcony, staring dry-eyed at the glittering water. Felix had gone into the bedroom and thrown himself on the bed. He stared up at the ceiling for a long time. Then he compressed his lips and clenched his fists. And then, with a scornful twist of his lips, he whispered, "Resignation! Resignation!"

From that moment on something had come between them, and at the same time they felt a nervous need to talk to each other a great deal. They discussed the most ordinary matters at length, and felt almost alarmed when the talking stopped. Where did those grey clouds above the mountains come from, what weather might they expect tomorrow, why was the water a different colour at different times of day? They held long conversations about such things. When they went out walking they strolled further from their house more often than they had done before, taking the path along the bank of the lake, where there were more buildings. That gave them many opportunities to discuss the people they met. If any young men happened to be coming towards them Marie was particularly reserved, and if Felix commented on the summer outfits of sportsmen, oarsmen or climbers, she went so far as to pretend—hardly aware that it was pretence at all—that she hadn't even noticed them, and she could only with difficulty be persuaded to observe them more closely if they met again. She found his look at such moments painfully embarrassing when she felt it resting on her. Then they might walk side by side in silence for quarter-of-an-hour. And sometimes they sat on the balcony without exchanging a word, until Marie often, but without any intention of hiding anything, as a last resort hit on reading aloud to him from the paper. Even when she saw that he wasn't listening any more she read on, glad to hear the sound of her own voice, glad not to have total silence between them. And yet in spite off all these efforts, which were a strain, they were both occupied solely with their own thoughts.

Felix confessed to himself that he had been acting out a ridiculous comedy for Marie's benefit. If he had been serious in his wish to spare her the coming misery, his best course would have been just to leave her. He could have found some quiet place to die in peace. He was surprised to find himself considering these questions with perfect indifference. But when he began seriously thinking how to execute such a plan, when he pictured all the details in his mind's eye during a terribly long, wakeful night—how he would get up and leave at dawn next day, without any goodbye, going alone to his imminent death and leaving Marie behind in the sunny, laughing life now lost to him—then he felt powerless, was profoundly convinced that he could not do it, would never be able to do it. So what now? The day when he *must* go and leave her behind was inexorably coming closer and closer. His whole existence was the expectation of that day, nothing but a painful respite, worse than death itself. If only he hadn't learned from youth onwards to observe himself! Then he could have ignored all the symptoms of his illness, or at least considered them minor troubles. His memory summoned up the images of people he had known who had been consumed by the same mortal sickness now consuming him, but who had been cheerfully looking to the future, full of hope, only a few weeks before they died. He cursed the hour when his uncertainty had taken him to the doctor whom he had badgered with lies and an assumption of false dignity until he learned the whole merciless truth. And so here he lay, damned a hundred times over, no better off than a prisoner condemned to death whom the hangman may lead to the place of execution any morning now, and he realised that he had never really for a moment been able to understand clearly the full horror of his present existence. In some remote corner of his heart there still lurked, treacherous and cajoling, the hope that refused ever to leave him entirely. But his reason was stronger, it gave him clear, cold counsel again and again, and he heard it ten, a hundred, a thousand times over in the endless nights when he lay awake, and during the monotonous days that none the less were passing too fast. It told him that there was only one way out, one thing that could save him: to stop waiting, not to wait an hour, a second longer, to make an end of it himself—that would be less pitiable. And it was almost a comfort to think that there was no compelling reason for him to wait. He could end it all at any time if he only wanted to.

But she, she! By day in particular, when she walked with him or read aloud to him, it often seemed as if it wouldn't be so difficult to part from this creature after all. She was no longer a part of his essential being. She belonged not to him but to the life all around him that he must leave. At other moments, however, particularly by night, when she lay fast asleep beside him in her youthful beauty, her eye-lids closed, he loved her immeasurably, and the more calmly she slept, the more remote from the world her slumbers, the further her dreaming soul seemed from his waking torment, the more madly he adored her. Once, on the night before they were to leave the lake, an almost irresistible desire came over him to wake her from her delicious sleep, which to him suggested malicious disloyalty, shake her and shout in her ear, "If you love me, then die with me, die now." But he let her sleep on. He would say it to her tomorrow, yes, tomorrow—perhaps.

She had sensed his eyes on her in those nights more often than he guessed. She had pretended to be asleep more often than he guessed, because a paralysing fear kept her from entirely opening her lids, though she sometimes peered through them in the half-light of the bedroom to see his figure sitting upright in the bed. The memory of that last grave conversation would not leave her, and she trembled at the thought of the day when he would ask her his question again. But why did it make her tremble? The answer was so obvious. She would stay with him to the last second, never leave his side, kiss every sigh from his lips, every tear of pain from his eyelashes! Did he doubt her? Was any other answer possible? How could it be? What answer? For instance: "You're right, I'll leave you. I'll just keep the memory of that interesting invalid. I'm leaving you on your own now so that I can love your memory better?" And then? She couldn't help picturing everything that must follow that answer. In her mind she sees him before her, cool, smiling. He stretches out his hand, saying, "Thank you". Then he turns away from her, and she hurries off. It's a summer morning, glowing with a thousand waking joys. And she hurries further and further into the golden dawn, just to get away from him as quickly as possible. Suddenly she isn't under a spell any more. She is alone again, free of pity. She no longer feels that look resting on her, the sad, questioning, dying look that has tormented her so terribly all these last months. She belongs to joy, to life, she can be young again. She hurries away, and the morning wind flutters after her, laughing … And how doubly miserable she seemed to herself when this picture surfaced in her troubled dreams! She suffered from the mere idea that she had ever seen it.

How pity for him gnawed her heart too, how she shuddered when she thought of what he knew and of his hopelessness! How she loved him, loved him more and more deeply the closer the day came when she must lose him! There could be no doubt of her answer. It was such a small thing to stay beside him and suffer with him! To see him waiting for death, share those months of mortal fear with him, that was so little! She wants to do more for him, she thinks, to give the best, the highest that she can. If she promised to kill herself on his grave he'd die doubting whether she would really do it. Die with him—no, she will die *before* him. When he asks, she will have the strength to say, "Let's bring this torment to an end! We'll die together, and we'll die now!" And even as this idea intoxicated her, she saw the woman whose picture had appeared to her just now—hurrying over the fields with the morning wind caressing her, running away towards life and joy, and saw that it was herself, a despicable, vile figure.

The day came when they had planned to leave. A wonderfully mild morning, as if spring were returning. Marie was already sitting on the balcony and breakfast was ready when Felix came out of the living-room. He took a deep breath. "Ah, what a lovely day!"

"Yes, isn't it?"

"I have something to say to you, Marie."

"What?" And she quickly went on, as if to take the words out of his mouth. "Oh, are we going to stay here a little longer?"

"Well, no, but we won't go straight back to Vienna. I don't feel bad today, not bad at all. We can stop somewhere on the way."

"Just as you like, darling." She suddenly felt happier deep inside her than she had for a long time. He hadn't spoken in so natural a tone of voice all that week.

"I thought we could stay in Salzburg, child."

"Anything you say."

"We'll still be back in Vienna soon enough, don't you think? And it would be rather a long railway journey for me."

"Well," said Marie briskly, "we're in no hurry."

"We're all packed, aren't we, sweetheart?"

"Oh, long ago. We can set off at once."

"I think we'll hire a carriage. It will be a drive of four or five hours, and much more comfortable than a rail journey. Yesterday's heat always lingers in the railway carriages."

"Just as you like, darling." She told him to drink his glass of milk, and then pointed out the beautiful, shimmering silver light on the crest of the waves. She talked a great deal, in bubbling high spirits. His replies were friendly and innocuous. At last she offered to go and order the carriage to come at midday and drive them to Salzburg. Smiling, he accepted this offer. She quickly put on her broad-brimmed straw hat, kissed Felix on the mouth a couple of times, and then went out into the road.

He hadn't asked his question—and he wasn't going to ask. She could see that clearly from his cheerful face. So there was nothing hidden behind his friendly manner today, as there sometimes was when he deliberately cut short an innocent conversation with a sharp remark. She had always known in advance when some such thing was coming, and now she felt as if he had shown her great mercy. There had been something generous, reconciliatory in his mild manner.

When she returned to the balcony she found him reading the newspaper which had arrived during her absence.

"Marie," he called, his glance telling her to come closer, "here's something strange, very strange."

"What is it?"

"Read this! That man—Professor Bernard, I mean—he's dead!"

"Who?"

"The man who—well, whom I—the doctor who gave me such a gloomy diagnosis."

She took the newspaper from him. "What, that Professor Bernard?" The remark 'It serves him right!' was on the tip of her tongue, but she bit it back. They both felt as if this incident held some special meaning for them. The very man who, in all the overweening wisdom of his own bounding good health, had taken all hope from the patient who came to him for help, had been carried away himself within a couple of days. Only now did

Felix understand how much he had hated the man—and the fact that Fate had taken such a sudden revenge seemed to the sick man a favourable sign. He felt as if an ominous ghost had ceased to haunt him. Marie threw the newspaper down and said, "Yes, indeed, what do we humans know of the future?"

He eagerly took up the idea. "What do we know of tomorrow? Nothing, nothing at all!" After a brief pause he suddenly changed the subject. "Did you order the carriage?"

"Yes," she said, "for eleven."

"Then we could take a little boat trip on the water first, couldn't we?"

She took his arm, and they both walked down to the boathouse with a sense of well-earned satisfaction.

Late that afternoon they drove into Salzburg. To their surprise, they found most of the buildings in the city flying flags; the people they met were in their best clothes, some wearing cockades. In the hotel where they took a room with a view of the Mönchsberg they heard that a great festival of vocal music was taking place in the city, and were offered tickets for the concert to be given at eight in the Kurpark, with magnificent illuminations. Their room was on the first floor, and the river Salzach flowed below their window. They had both dropped off to sleep during the drive, and now felt so refreshed that they spent only a short time indoors, and went out into the streets again before dusk.

There was a cheerful, lively mood all over the city. Almost all the people of Salzburg seemed to be out in the streets, and the singers, adorned with their cockades, were walking among them in merry groups. There were many foreigners around too, and visitors had come in even from the surrounding villages, pushing their way through the crowd in their rustic Sunday clothes. Flags in the city colours flew from the gables, triumphal arches decked with flowers had been erected in the main thoroughfares, a restless torrent of human beings surged through all the streets, and the sky of a fragrant summer evening spread above them, comfortably mild.

From the banks of the Salzach, where pleasant silence surrounded them, Felix and Marie had reached the more hectic hurry and bustle of the city centre, and after spending such a quiet time in their lakeside retreat all the unaccustomed noise almost confused them. But they had soon recovered the confidence of city dwellers, and allowed the scene to make its effect on them. Felix was not very pleasantly struck by the cheerfulness of the crowd—well, that had always been his way. Marie, however, soon seemed to feel very much at home, and like a child she stopped now and then to look first at some women in Salzburg costume, then at a party of tall male singers adorned with sashes who were strolling past. Sometimes she glanced up and admired the particularly handsome decoration of a building. From time to time she turned to Felix, who was walking beside her rather listlessly, with a lively "Do look, how pretty!" and received no answer but a silent nod of his head.

"Seriously, do tell me," she said at last, "weren't we lucky to come just now?"

He looked at her with an expression which she couldn't quite interpret. At last he said, "I suppose you'd like to go to that concert in the Kurpark too?"

She only smiled, and then replied, "Well, we don't have to go out at once!"

That smile irritated him. "I do believe you really would expect it of me!"

"Oh, what are you thinking of?" she cried in alarm, and at the same time her eyes wandered to the other side of the street, where an elegant, good-looking couple who looked like honeymooners were just walking past in smiling conversation. Marie walked on beside Felix, but without taking his arm. Quite often the crowd parted them for a few seconds, and then she found him keeping close to the walls of the buildings, obviously reluctant to come into more direct contact with all the people. Meanwhile it was getting darker, the street lights were coming on, and coloured lanterns had been put up here and there around the city, particularly on the triumphal arches,. The main throng was making for the Kurhaus. It would soon be time for the concert. At first Felix and Marie were carried along by the crowd, then he suddenly took her arm and, turning into a narrow side street, they were soon in a quieter and less brightly lit district. After walking along in silence for a few minutes, they found themselves in a remote place on the banks of the Salzach, where the monotonous sound of the river rushing by rose to them.

"What are we going to do here?" she asked.

"Rest," he said in an almost peremptory tone. And when she did not reply, he went on in a voice of nervous agitation "We don't belong there. Coloured lights, cheerful singing, the company of people who are young and laughing aren't for us now. *This* is the place for us, where we won't hear any of the rejoicing and can be alone; this is where we belong." And then, lapsing from that agitated tone into one of cold scorn: "Or at least, where *I* belong."

As he said that, she felt that she was not as deeply moved as usual, but she explained it by telling herself that she had often heard him say such things when he was obviously exaggerating. She replied, in a mild and conciliatory tone, "I don't deserve that, I really don't."

But he, as so often before, retorted sarcastically "Oh, do forgive me."

She went on, holding his arm and pressing it, "We *neither* of us belong here."

"Yes, we do!" he almost screamed.

"No," she gently replied. "I don't want to go back and join all those crowds either. I disliked them just as much as you did. But why should we run away as if we were outcasts?"

At that moment a full orchestral sound rang out, making its way to them through the pure, windless air. They could hear it clearly, almost note by note. The trombone played solemn fanfares; it was a festival overture clearly designed to open the concert.

"Let's go," said Felix suddenly, after standing with her and listening for a while. "Music heard from a distance makes me sadder than almost anything else on earth."

"Yes," she agreed, "it does sound very melancholy."

They walked quickly towards the city. Here the music was not as distinct as down by the river-bank, and when they were back in the brightly lit streets full of people Marie felt her old affectionate pity for her lover return. She understood how he felt again, she forgave him everything. "Shall we go back to the hotel?" she asked.

"No, why? Are you sleepy?"

"Oh no!"

"Then let's stay out-of-doors a little longer, shall we?"

"Of course—if you'd like to. Are you sure it's not too cool for you?"

"This is sultry weather. Positively hot" he replied fretfully. "Let's eat out in the open."

"That would be very nice."

They were approaching the Kurpark. The orchestra had finished its overture, and now all the hundreds of sounds made by a crowd of people talking cheerfully could be heard from the park, which was illuminated as brightly as if it were day. A few people still on their way to the concert hurried past. Two male singers, arriving late, quickly overtook them too. Marie looked at them as they went by, and next moment, not without some anxiety and as if she must atone for some misdemeanour, she looked at Felix. He was gnawing his lip, and a look of carefully repressed irritation could be read on his brow. She thought he was sure to say something, but he did not. And his sombre glance turned away from her and back to the two men just disappearing through the entrance to the park. He knew his own feelings. There before him went what he most hated. A part of what would be still here when *he* was gone, would still be young and lively, would laugh when he couldn't laugh or weep any more. Here beside him, now pressing closer to his arm than before in the knowledge of her guilt, walked another such specimen of laughing, living youth, unconsciously feeling a relationship with those men. And *he* knew it; it churned around in his mind with raging pain. For several long seconds neither of them said anything. At last he sighed deeply. She tried to see his face, but he had turned it away. Suddenly he said "This would be all right."

At first she didn't know what he meant. "What would?"

They were standing outside a garden restaurant close to the Kurpark, with tall trees spreading above tables with white covers, and a few lighted lanterns. There were not many guests here. They had plenty of tables to choose from, and finally settled in a corner of the garden. There were barely twenty people in the place. Close to them sat the elegant young couple whom they had already seen once that day. Marie recognised them at once. A chorus was beginning over in the park. Slightly muted, but very melodious, the voices came to their ears, and it was as if the leaves of the trees moved as the mighty echo of cheerful song passed over them. Felix had ordered a good Rhine wine, and he sat there with his eyes half-closed, relishing the wine on his tongue and giving way to the magic of the music without troubling any more about its source. Marie had moved close to him, and he felt the warmth of her knee beside his. After the terrible agitation of the last few minutes a kind of indifference had come over him, doing him good, and he was glad that he had forced himself to feel that indifference. For as soon as they sat down at the table he had firmly resolved to overcome the sharp pain he felt. He was too exhausted to wonder more closely how far his will had helped him to do so. Now, however, many considerations soothed his feelings: perhaps he had read more and worse into that look of Marie's than it deserved, perhaps she would have glanced at anyone else in just the same way, and indeed she was now observing the two strangers at the next table exactly as she had looked at those singers a little earlier.

The wine was good, the pleasing music drifted their way, the summer evening was intoxicatingly mild, and as Felix looked at Marie he saw the light of endless love and kindness in her eyes. He wished he could immerse himself entirely into the present moment. He made one final demand on his will, to free himself from all that was the past or the future. He wanted to be happy, or at least drunk. And suddenly, quite unexpectedly, an entirely new and wonderfully liberating sensation came to him: he felt that now it would barely cost him any determination at all to end his life. To end it now. And that option was always open; his present mood could easily be induced again. Music, to be slightly tipsy with a sweet girl beside him— oh yes, it was Marie. He thought. Perhaps any other girl would have been as dear to him just now. She too was sipping the wine with pleasure. Felix would soon have to order another bottle. He felt more content than he had been for a long time. He told himself that, fundamentally, all this was to be put down to a little more alcohol than he usually drank. But what did that matter, if he could feel like this? Truly, death held no more terrors for him. Nothing mattered.

"Don't you agree, sweetheart?" he said.

She moved close to him. "What did you want to know?"

"Nothing matters, don't you agree?"

"Yes," she said, "except that I love you for ever and ever."

It seemed to him very strange that she should say that so gravely just now. He was hardly aware of her as a person. She merged with everything else. Yes, this was the way, this was how to handle it. No, it's not the wine talking, he thought, wine simply liberates us from what usually makes us plodding and cowardly—it drains their importance from people and things. A little white powder, now, tip it into the glass—how simple that would be! As he thought this he felt a few tears come to his eyes. He was slightly moved by himself.

Over in the park the chorus ended. They could hear the applause and cries of "Bravo!" and then the orchestra struck up again, this time the measured merriment of a polonaise. Felix beat time with his hand. A thought passed through his mind: I'll live what little life is left as well as I can. There was nothing terrible in that idea, rather something proud and royal. What, wait in fear for the last breath, a moment that is certain to come to everyone? Spoil his days and nights with empty brooding, he thinks, when he feels to his innermost being that he is still capable and strong enough for all kinds of pleasures, when he's aware of the music inspiring him, the wine that tastes delicious, when he'd like to take this glowing girl on his lap and cover her with kisses? No, it's too soon yet to let himself feel embittered! And when the hour does come in which nothing inspires him, in which desire does not exist for him any more—then a quick end made of his own free will, proud and kingly! He took Marie's hand and held it in his own for a long time, letting his breath waft slowly over her.

"Ah," whispered Marie, with a look of contentment.

He scrutinized her at length. And she was beautiful—beautiful! "Come on" he said. "Let's go."

"Why don't we listen to another song?" she ingenuously replied.

"Yes, yes," he said. "We'll open our window and let the wind carry the song into our room."

"Are you feeling tired now?" she asked, with a little anxiety.

He stroked her hair, laughing. "Yes."

"Then let's go."

They rose and left the garden. She took his arm, clung fast to it, and leaned her cheek against his shoulder. On their way back the two of them were accompanied by the ever-receding sound of the chorus, which the solo singers had just joined. The music was cheerful, in waltz time with a high-spirited refrain, so that they were obliged to walk more lightly and easily. The hotel was only a few minutes away. As they climbed the steps the sound of the music died away, but no sooner were they in their room than the refrain of the waltz song met their ears again, as merry as ever.

They found the window wide open, and blue moon-light flooding softly in. Opposite, the Mönchsberg and the fortress on it were sharply outlined. There was no need for a light, since a broad strip of silver moonlight lay over the floor, leaving only the corners of the room still dark. In one of them, close to the window, stood an armchair. Felix dropped into it and pulled Marie firmly to him. He kissed her, she kissed him back. Over in the park the song had ended, but the applause went on and on until the singers began all over again. Suddenly Marie rose and hastened to the window. Felix followed her. "What is it?" he asked.

"No, no!"

He stamped his foot. "What do you mean, no?"

"Felix!" Beseechingly, she folded her hands.

"No?" he said through compressed lips. "No? You think I ought to be preparing to die with dignity?"

"Oh, Felix!" And she was down on the floor in front of him, clasping his knees.

He raised her to her feet. "You're such a child," he whispered, and then into her ear, "I love you, did you know? And we'll be happy as long as this little bit of life lasts. I don't want a year spent in fear and trembling, I'd rather have just a few weeks, a few days and nights, but I want to live them fully, I won't deny myself anything, anything, and then—well, down there, if you like." And as he stood with one arm round her, he pointed with the other to the window, where the river flowed past. The singers had ended their song, and now they could hear the quiet rushing of the water.

Marie did not reply. She had both hands clasped behind his neck, and Felix drank in the fragrance of her hair. How he adored her! Yes, a few more days of happiness, and then …

All was quiet around them, and Marie had fallen asleep beside him. The concert was over long ago, and below their window the last straggling members of the audience were walking by, talking and laughing loudly. And Felix thought how strange it was that these noisy people could well be the same whose singing had moved him so deeply. Even the last voices finally died away, and now he heard only the melancholy flowing of the river. Yes, just a few more days and nights, and then—but she was too fond of life. Would she ever dare to do it? Though she needn't dare anything, needn't even know anything. The time will come, he thinks, when she falls asleep in his arms, as she is sleeping now—and never wakes up again. And when he is quite sure of that then—yes, *then* he too can be gone. But he won't say anything to her, she likes living too much! She'd be afraid of him, and then in the end he'll have to be alone as he—oh, a terrible thought! It would be best to do it now, at once—she's sleeping so soundly! A little firm pressure here on her throat, and it's done. But no, how stupid. He has many hours of happiness ahead of him first; he'll know which must be the last.

He looked at Marie, and felt as if he were holding his sleeping slave-girl in his arms.

The decision he had finally made soothed him. Over the next few days, a smile of glee played around his mouth as he walked through the streets with Marie and sometimes saw a man's eyes rest admiringly on her. And when they went out together, when they sat in a garden in the evening, when he held her in a close embrace at night, he felt more pride of possession than ever before. Only one thing sometimes troubled him, and that was that she wouldn't be going with him of her own free will. But he saw indications that he could achieve that too. She no longer ventured to reject his stormy desires, she had never before abandoned herself to him as wonderfully as she had these last few nights, and with trembling joy he saw the moment approach when he would dare to tell her, "We will die today". However, he kept putting that moment off. Sometimes he saw a picture in his mind painted in romantic colours: he himself driving a dagger into her heart, she kissing his beloved hand as she breathed her last. He kept asking himself if the moment had come yet, and he still wasn't sure.

One morning Marie woke and was severely alarmed: Felix wasn't beside her. She sat up in bed, and then she saw him sitting in the armchair by the window, pale as death, his head sunk on his chest, his shirt open. In the grip of dreadful fear, she ran to him. "Felix!"

He opened his eyes. "What? Where?" Then he clutched his chest and groaned.

"Why didn't you wake me?" she cried, wringing her hands.

"It's all right now," he said. She hurried over to the bed, took the blanket off it and spread it over his knees.

"For Heaven's sake, how did you get here?" she asked.

"I don't know. I must have been dreaming. Something seized me by the throat, and I couldn't breathe. I never thought of you! Breathing is easier here by the window."

Marie had quickly put on a dress and closed the window, for an uncomfortable wind had risen, and now fine rain began to fall from the grey sky, bringing chilly, damp air into the room. Suddenly all the comfortable intimacy of the summer night was gone, the place was grey and strange. All at once a cheerless autumn morning was here, dispelling the magic that they had dreamed into the place.

Felix was perfectly calm. "Why do you look so alarmed? What's the matter? I've always had bad dreams, even when I was in good health."

There was no pacifying her. "Please, Felix, let's go back, let's go home to Vienna."

"But—"

"Summer's over now anyway. Just look out of the window—it's all so bleak and unwelcoming! And it could be dangerous if the weather is turning cold."

He listened attentively. To his own surprise, at this moment he felt very well, like a tired convalescent. His breath came easily, and there was something sweet and soothing in his weariness. He liked the idea of leaving Salzburg. The thought of a change of place appealed to him. He looked forward to reclining in their compartment of the railway carriage, this cool, rainy day with his head on Marie's breast.

"Good," he said, "let's leave."

"Today?"

"Yes, today. By the noon express, if you like."

"But won't that tire you?"

"Oh, what ideas you take into your head! The journey won't be any strain, why would it be? And you'll deal with anything that might trouble me, won't you?"

She was immensely glad to have brought him round so easily to the idea of leaving, and immediately set about packing. She saw to paying their bill, ordered a cab, and reserved a compartment on the train. Felix was soon dressed, but did not leave the room, and spent all morning lying on the sofa. He watched Marie hurrying busily around, and sometimes smiled. But most of the time he slept. He was so tired, so tired, and when he looked at her he was glad to think of her staying with him everywhere he went. And the thought that they would rest together went through his head, as if in a dream. "Soon, soon," he thought, yet the moment had never seemed to him so far away.

So that afternoon, just as he had pictured it earlier, Felix lay in the compartment of the railway carriage, comfortably stretched out full length, his head on Marie's breast, the rug spread over him. He stared through the closed window panes at the grey day outside, saw the rain falling, and let his eyes wander to the mist from which nearby hills and buildings sometimes emerged. Telegraph poles shot by, their wires dancing up and down, now and then the train stopped at a station, but from where he lay Felix couldn't make out any passengers on the platform. He heard only the muted sounds of footsteps, voices, bells ringing, train horns giving signals. At first he asked Marie to read him the paper, but she had to raise her voice too much, and soon they gave up the attempt. They were both glad to be going home.

Dusk was gathering, and still the rain fell. Felix needed to think perfectly clearly, but his ideas refused to take distinct shape. He fell into reflective mood. So here we have a man who's severely ill ... he's been staying in the mountains, because that's where severely ill people go in summer ... and there's his mistress, who has cared for him faithfully, but now she's tired ... She looks so pale, or is that just the light? ... Ah, yes, the overhead lighting is on. But it isn't entirely dark outside yet ... And now autumn is coming ... autumn, such a sad, quiet time ... We'll be back at home in Vienna this evening ... And then I'll feel as if I'd never been away ... It's just as well that Marie is asleep. I wouldn't want to listen to her talking now ... I wonder if there are any people from that festival of vocal music on this train? I'm tired, that's all, not ill. There are a great many passengers in a worse way than me on the train ... It's good to be alone ... How has this whole day passed? Was it really today that I was lying on the sofa in Salzburg? It's so long ago ... ah, what do we know about time and space? ... the mystery of the world, perhaps we'll solve it when we die ... And now a melody sounded in his ear. He knew it was only the sound of the moving train, yet it was a melody ... A folk-song, a Russian song ... monotonous ... very beautiful ...

"Felix, Felix!"

"What is it?"

Marie was standing in front of him, caressing his cheeks. "Did you sleep well, Felix?"

"What is it?"

"We'll be in Vienna in a quarter-of-an-hour's time."

"Oh, I don't believe it!"

"You had a really healthy sleep. I'm sure it's done you good."

She put their baggage in order as the train rushed on through the night. Every minute now they heard a shrill, long-drawn-out whistle, while lights flashed in through the window from outside and quickly died away again. They were passing through the stations near Vienna.

Felix sat up. "I feel quite tired from lying down so long," he said. He sat in the corner and looked out of the window. From afar, he could already see the glow over the city streets. The train was going more slowly now; Marie opened the compartment window and leaned out. They came into the station, and Marie waved out of the window. Then she turned to Felix, saying, "There he is, there he is."

"Who?"

"Alfred!"

"Alfred?"

She was still waving. Felix had risen to his feet and was looking over her shoulder. Alfred quickly came over to their compartment and reached his hand up to Marie. "Good evening! Hello, Felix."

"How do you come to be here?"

"I sent him a telegram," Marie was quick to reply. "To say we were coming."

"A nice kind of friend you are!" Alfred told him. 'I suppose letter-writing is an unknown invention so far as you're concerned. Well, come along now!"

"I've slept so much," said Felix, "I still feel quite muzzy." He smiled as he climbed down the steps from the carriage, swaying slightly.

Alfred took one of his arms, and Marie, as if just to link arms with him, quickly took the other.

"You must both be very tired, I'm sure."

"I'm worn to a shred!" said Marie. "All this tedious train travelling leaves one tired out, doesn't it, Felix?"

Slowly, they went down the steps from the station. Marie was trying to catch Alfred's eye, he avoided her glance. At the bottom of the steps he hailed a cab. "I'm glad to have seen you, my dear Felix," he said. "I'll come round in the morning, and we'll have a good long chat."

"I feel all muzzy," repeated Felix. Alfred tried to help him into the cab. "Oh, not as bad as that, dear me, no!" He got in and reached his hand out to Marie. "There, you see?" Marie followed him.

"We'll see you tomorrow, then," she said, giving Alfred her hand in farewell through the cab window. There was such questioning fear in her eyes that Alfred forced himself to smile.

"Yes, tomorrow," he called. "I'll come to breakfast with you!" And the cab drove away. Alfred stood where he was for a while, his face grave.

"My poor friend!" he whispered to himself.

Next morning Alfred arrived very early, and Marie met him at the door. "I must talk to you," she said.

"Let me go in and see him first. Everything we have to discuss will make more sense after I've examined him."

"I want to ask you just one thing, Alfred! However you find him, I beg you, don't tell him anything!"

"What are you thinking of? Come on, it won't be as bad as all that. Is he still asleep?"

"No, he's awake."

"What kind of night did he have?"

"He slept until four in the morning. After that he was restless."

"Leave me alone with him first. You must get a little peace into that pale little face of yours. You can't go in to him like that." Smiling, he pressed her hand, and entered the bedroom alone. Felix had drawn the covers up to his chin, and nodded at his friend. Alfred sat down on the edge of the bed, saying, "Well, it's good to have you home again. You've recovered splendidly, and I hope you left your melancholy behind in the mountains."

"Oh yes!" replied Felix. His expression was unchanged.

"Sit up a moment, please. I make such early visits only in my medical capacity."

"Very well," said Felix indifferently.

Alfred examined the invalid, asked some questions that Felix answered briefly, and finally said "Well, we can be reasonably satisfied so far."

"Don't try deceiving me," replied Felix morosely.

"And don't you persist in foolishness. We want to attack this thing head on. You must summon up the will to get better, stop acting the part of a man resigned to his fate. It doesn't suit you."

"So what do you suggest I do?"

"First of all, stay in bed for a few days, understand?"

"I don't feel like getting up anyway."

"That's all to the good."

Felix became more animated. "There's just one thing I'd like to know. What happened to me yesterday? Seriously, Alfred, you must explain it to me. It's all like a vague dream. The train journey, arriving, how I came up here and found myself in bed … "

"What is there to explain? You don't have a giant's strength, and when you're overtired it's easy to account for such things!"

"No, Alfred. Weariness such as I felt yesterday is something quite new to me. I'm still tired today, but I can think clearly again. Yesterday wasn't so very unpleasant, but I don't like remembering it. When I think that something of the kind could happen to me again—"

At this moment Marie entered the room.

"Well, you have Alfred to thank for this," Felix told her. "He's appointing you sick-nurse. I'm to lie here from now on. I have the honour of presenting you to my deathbed."

Marie looked horrified.

"Don't let this idiot bewilder you," said Alfred. "He has to stay in bed for a few days, and I'm sure you'll be kind enough to look after him."

"Oh, Alfred, you have no idea what a ministering angel I have at my side," cried Felix with heavy sarcasm.

Alfred gave her extensive instructions on the way to nurse and care for Felix, and finally said, "I'm telling you now, my dear Felix, I'll come to see you as a doctor only every other day. That's all you need. And we won't say a word about your condition on the days in between. I'll visit just to talk to you as usual then."

"Good God," cried Felix, "what a psychologist the man is! You can keep those tricks for your other patients, particularly the more simple-minded among them."

"Felix, I'm talking to you man to man, so listen. It is true that you're ill. But it's also true that with proper nursing you'll get better. I can't say any more or any less than that." With these words, he rose to his feet.

Felix's eyes followed him with suspicion. "One might almost be tempted to believe him."

"That's up to you, my dear Felix," replied the Doctor briefly.

"There, Alfred, now you've given yourself away again," said the sick man. "That brusque manner to the severely ill—everyone knows that trick."

"I'll see you tomorrow," said Alfred, turning to the door. Marie followed, and was going to accompany him out. "No, stay there," he whispered in a peremptory tone. She closed the door behind him as he left.

"Come here, little one!" said Felix as she busied herself at the table with her needlework, a cheerful smile on her face. "Yes, here. There, you're a good, good, very good girl." These affectionate words were spoken in a sharp, bitter tone.

For the next few days Marie never moved from his bed-side, and was full of kindness and devotion; she radiated a quiet, unaffected cheerfulness that was meant to do the invalid good, and sometimes really did. Often, however, he was irritated by the gentle good humour with which Marie tried to surround him, and then, when she began chattering about some piece of news in the paper, or saying she thought he looked better or talking of their future life once he really *was* better, he would interrupt, asking her to be good enough to leave him alone and spare him all that stuff. Alfred called daily, sometimes twice a day, but hardly seemed to be troubled about his friend's physical state. He spoke of mutual friends, told stories about the hospital, and embarked upon artistic and literary discussions, although taking care that Felix wasn't called upon to say too much. Both his lover and his friend acted so naturally that Felix sometimes had difficulty in defending himself against the audacious hopes that forced themselves upon him. He told himself that those two were only doing their duty in acting out the comedy always performed, with varying degrees of success, for the benefit of the very ill. But although he thought he was simply going along with them and act-ing in the play too, he often found himself talking of the world and other people as if he were destined to spend many more years in the sunlight, among the living. And then he remembered that exactly this strange sense of well-being was often said to be a sign of the approaching end in victims of his own illness, and bitterly rejected all hope. He even reached the point where he thought vague anxious feelings and dark moods were a good sign, and almost felt glad of them. Then he thought how senseless that kind of logic was—only to realise at last that there could be no knowledge and no certainty in his case. He had begun reading again, but couldn't enjoy novels; they bored him, and many, particularly those offering a long-term view of a flourishing future full of incident, left him in a dark mood. He turned to philosophers, and asked Marie to take Schopenhauer and Nietzsche out of the bookshelves for him. But their wisdom brought him peace only for a short while.

One evening Alfred found him just as he had lowered a volume of Schopenhauer to his bedspread, and was staring straight ahead of him with a gloomy expression. Marie was sitting beside him, busy with some needlework.

"I'll tell you something, Alfred," he told the visitor with an almost agitated voice. "I'm going to go back to reading fiction."

"What's all this about?"

"Well, at least they're honest storytelling, good or bad, about artists or failures. But these gentlemen," and he glanced at the volume lying on his bed, "are shocking *poseurs.*"

"I see!"

Felix sat up in bed. "Despising life when you're as healthy as a god, looking death calmly in the eye when you're walking around Italy and life around you is blooming in the brightest of colours—that's what I call posturing. Shut one of those gentlemen up in a bedroom, condemn him to be feverish and breathless, tell him he's going to be buried some time between the first of January and the first of February next year. And then get him to philosophize to you!"

"Oh, come on," said Alfred. "What kind of paradox is that?"

"You don't understand. You can't understand! But it nauseates me. *Poseurs*, all of them!"

"What about Socrates?"

"A play-actor. A man behaving naturally fears the unknown, and at the very best he contrives to hide it. I'll tell you straight out, people falsify the psychology of the dying, because all the great figures of world history of whose deaths we know anything felt duty-bound to put on an act for posterity. And what about me? What am I doing? Yes, what? If I talk calmly to you about all kinds of things that are no longer anything to do with me, what exactly am I doing?"

"Come on, don't talk so much, particularly not such nonsense."

"I too feel in duty bound to pretend, whereas in reality I'm prey to a boundless, raging fear of a kind that healthy people can't imagine. They're all afraid, and that includes the heroes and the philosophers, only they make the best play-actors."

"Do calm down, Felix," Marie begged him.

"And I expect," the invalid continued, "you two, like all the rest, believe you can look eternity steadily in the eye, but that's because you have no real idea of it yet. You have to be condemned, like a criminal—or like me, then you can talk about it. As for the poor devil who goes to the gallows with composure, the great sage who thinks up maxims after draining the cup of hemlock, the captured freedom fighter smiling as he sees the guns levelled at his chest, they're all pretending, *I* know they are—I know their composure, their smiles are a pose, because they're all afraid, horribly afraid of death. It's as natural as dying itself."

Alfred had sat down on the bed calmly, and when Felix had finished he replied, "Be that as it may, first it's not sensible of you to talk so much and in such a loud voice. And second, you're as tasteless as all-be-damned and a terrible hypochondriac!"

"Just now, when you're doing so well!" cried Marie.

"Does she really think so, after all?" asked Felix, turning to Alfred. "Do please explain to her, will you?"

"My dear friend," replied the Doctor, "you're the one who needs an explanation. But you're being wilful today, and I must decline to give one. In two or three days, as long as you don't launch into any more long speeches, you'll probably be fit to get up, and then we'll have a proper discussion of your state of mind."

"If only I didn't see through you so clearly," said Felix.

"Very well, very well," replied Alfred. "Don't look so upset," he added, to Marie. "Even our friend here will see reason again some time. And now, why aren't there any windows open here? It's a perfect autumn day outside."

Marie rose and opened a window. Dusk was just beginning to fall, and the air that came in was so refreshing that she longed to let it caress her for longer. She stayed by the window, leaning out. Suddenly she felt as if she had left the room itself. She might have been out-of-doors on her own; it was many days since she had experienced such a pleasant sensation. Now, as she put her head back into the room, the musty sickroom atmosphere met her and lay oppressively on her breast. She saw Felix and Alfred talking and couldn't make out the exact words, but there was no need for her to take part in their conversation. Once again she leaned out. The road was quiet and empty, and only the muted sound of passing carriages came from the nearby main street. A few people out walking strolled along the pavement at their leisure. A couple of servant girls were standing at the entrance of the building opposite, talking and laughing. Like Marie herself, a young woman in that building was looking out of a window. At that moment Marie couldn't imagine why the young woman didn't go for a walk instead. She envied all these people; they were all happier than she was.

September brought mild and pleasant days. The evenings came early but were warm, without any wind.

Marie had fallen into the habit of moving her chair away from the invalid's bedside and sitting by the open window as often as she could. She could sit there for hours, particularly when Felix was asleep. Deep fatigue had come over her, an inability to be perfectly clear in her mind about what was going on, indeed a pronounced disinclination to think much at all. There were hours on end when she entertained neither memories nor ideas of the future. She was dreaming with her eyes open, and was glad when a little fresh air wafted into her face from the street. Then, when she caught a faint moan from the sickbed, she woke with a start. She realised that the gift of sympathy had gradually left her. Her pity had turned to nervous strain, her grief to mingled fear and indifference. She certainly had nothing to reproach herself for, and when the doctor in all seriousness called her an angel, as he had done recently, she need hardly feel ashamed. Yet she was tired, infinitely tired. It was ten or twelve days since she had been out of the house. Why? Why? She had to think about it. Well, of course, the thought came to her like a flash of inspiration, because it would have wounded Felix, that was why! And she was happy to stay with him, of course. She adored him no less than before. It was just that she was tired, and that was only human. And her longing for a few hours out-of-doors became stronger and stronger. She was being childish in denying herself its satisfaction. Felix himself ought to understand, after all. And now she realised yet again how infinitely she must love him, since she wanted to keep even the vaguest sense of injury away from him. She had let her needlework slip to the floor, and glanced at the bed, which now lay entirely in the shadow of the bedroom wall. It was dusk, and the sick man had fallen asleep after a quieter day. She could actually have gone out now, and he would have known nothing about it. Oh, to go down into the street, and then around the corner, and be among other people again, walk on to the

Stadtpark and then to the Ring, past the bright lights of the opera house in the middle of a busy crowd of people—and she longed so much to be in that crowd! But when would she know anything like that again? It could only be when Felix was better, and what were the street and the park and other human beings to her, what was life itself to her without him?

She stayed at home. She moved her chair close to his bed, took the sleeping man's hand and wept sad, quiet tears over it, and she was still weeping when her thoughts had long ago strayed from the man on whose pale hand her tears fell.

When Alfred visited Felix next day he found him better than he had been for a few days past. "If this goes on," he told him "I'll let you get up in a day or so." The invalid received this with suspicion, as he did everything said to him now, answering with a morose "Yes, yes." Alfred, however, turned to Marie, who was seated at the table, and said, "I'd like to see you looking a little better yourself."

Even Felix, who looked more closely at Marie on hearing these words, noticed how very pale she was. He was used to quickly dismissing those thoughts of her self-sacrificing kindness that sometimes crossed his mind. At times he suspected that her martyrdom was not entirely genuine and felt upset by the patient manner she wore, just for show. At other times he wished she would be impatient. He was waiting for the moment when she would give herself away with a word, a look, and he could angrily throw the facts in her face: he hadn't been taken in for a moment, her hypocrisy revolted him, she'd better leave him to die in peace. Now that Alfred had mentioned her appearance she flushed slightly, and smiled. "I'm feeling perfectly well," she said.

Alfred came closer to her. "It's not as simple as that. Your Felix won't have much joy of his recovery if you're the next to fall ill yourself."

"But I really am well."

"Tell me, are you getting any little fresh air?"

"I truly don't feel the need for it."

"Felix, you tell me—is she with you all the time?"

"You know she is," said Felix. "She's an angel."

"Forgive me for saying so, Marie, but that's just plain stupid. It's useless, childish to put such a strain on yourself. You must get some air. It's necessary, I prescribe it."

"Oh, what do you want me to do?" asked Marie, with a faint smile. "I assure you that I don't feel I need it."

"Never mind that. If you don't feel you need it, that's a bad sign too. You must go out today. Sit in the park for an hour. Or if you don't feel happy about that, take a cab and go for a drive, around the Prater, for instance. It's wonderful there at the moment."

"But—"

"No buts. If you go on like this, if you're a ministering angel all the time, you'll ruin your health. Take a look in the mirror. I tell you, you'll ruin your health."

As Alfred said this Felix felt a sharp pang go to his

heart. Grim anger raged in him. He thought he saw an expression of deliberate endurance inviting sympathy on her face, and it went through his mind, like an irrefutable truth, that this woman had undertaken to suffer with him, die with him. She'll ruin her health? Well, yes, of course. Did she intend to go about with pink cheeks and shining eyes while he himself hastened towards his end? And does Alfred really believe, Felix thought, that the woman who is his lover has any right to think beyond the hour that would be his last? Will she herself perhaps dare—

With avid rage, Felix studied the expression on Marie's face while the doctor kept repeating what he had just said in a tone of displeasure. At last he induced Marie to promise that she would go out for a breath of fresh air today, explaining that keeping this promise was as much part of her nursing duties as all the rest. Yes, because I don't count any more, thought Felix. Because they might as well leave a man who's done for anyway to get worse and worse. He shook hands apathetically with Alfred when his friend left at last. He hated him.

Marie went no further than the bedroom door with the doctor, and then came straight back to Felix. He was lying there with his lips compressed and a deep furrow of anger on his brow. She understood him, she understood him so well. Leaning down, she smiled at him. He took a deep breath, wanting to speak, to fling some outrageous insult in her face. He felt as if she deserved it. But she, stroking his hair and still with that tired, patient smile on her face, whispered lovingly, very close to his lips, "I won't go out." He did not reply. She sat at his bedside all through that long evening and until far into the night, when at last she fell asleep in her chair.

When Alfred called next day, Marie tried to avoid talking to him. But he didn't seem interested in her own appearance today, and turned all his attention to Felix. He said no more about getting up soon, and the invalid felt reluctant to ask him. He was feeling weaker than he had for a few days, and less like talking than ever; he was glad when the doctor had left, and gave only curt, fretful answers to Marie's questions. When, after hours of silence, she asked late in the afternoon "How are you feeling now?" he replied, "What does it matter?" He had clasped his hands above his head, he closed his eyes, and soon fell asleep. Marie stayed beside him for some time, watching him, and then her thoughts blurred and she drifted into dreams. When she woke up again some time later, she felt a curiously pleasant sensation flowing through her limbs, as if she had been roused from a sound, deep sleep. She got to her feet and raised the window blinds, which had been lowered. It was as if the fragrance of late flowers had wandered into the narrow street from the nearby park today. The air flooding into the room had never seemed to her so wonderful before. She looked round at Felix, who lay there still sleeping, breathing peacefully. At such moments, she normally felt an emotional impulse that kept her spellbound in the room, permeated by a sense of dull melancholy. Today she was calm, was pleased that Felix was sleeping, and without any inner struggle, as naturally as if it happened every day. She came to the decision to spend an hour out-of-doors. Going into the kitchen on tiptoe, she asked the maid to sit in the sickroom for a while, quickly picked up her hat and parasol, and flew rather than walked downstairs. Now she was out in the street. After walking quickly down a couple of quiet alleys she reached the park and was glad to see the shrubs and trees beside her, and above her the dusky blue sky she had longed for so much. She sat down on a bench. Nursemaids and maidservants sat on the benches near her, and small children were playing in the avenues. But as dusk was falling there would soon be an end to all this activity. The nursemaids called to their charges, took their hands and left the park. Soon Marie was almost alone, except for a few people still passing by, and now and then a gentleman turned to look at her.

So here she was in the open air. What was her situation now? For this seemed to her the moment to survey the present with an undisturbed eye. She wanted to find clear words for her thoughts, words that she could utter in her mind. I am with him because I love him. I'm not making any sacrifice, because there's nothing else I can do. And what will happen now? How much longer will it be? There's no hope for him. And then what? Then what? I once wanted to die with him. Why are we such strangers to each other now? He thinks only of himself. Does *he* still want to die with *me*? The certainty came to her that he did. But what she saw was not the picture of a loving young man who wished to have her lying in bed beside him for all eternity. It was more as if he were forcibly, jealously dragging her down because she belonged to him.

A young man had seated himself on the bench beside her and made some remark or other. Her mind was so distracted that at first she said: "What did you say?" Then she rose and moved quickly away. She found the glances of the people she met in the park uncomfortable. Going out into the Ring, she hailed a cab and went for a drive. It was evening now, she leaned comfortably back in a corner of the cab and enjoyed its pleasant, easy motion and the various sights she saw, bathed in dusk and the flickering light of the gas lamps as they passed by. The beautiful September evening had tempted many people into the street. As Marie was driven past the Volksgarten she heard the brisk notes of a military band playing, and involuntarily thought of that evening in Salzburg. She tried in vain to persuade herself that all this life around her was paltry, ephemeral, she would have no difficulty about leaving it. But she couldn't dispel the sense of well-being that was gradually filling her. She felt well, that was it. Everything did her good: the festive look of the theatre with its bright white arc lighting, people strolling at their ease out of the avenues of the Rathaus park and along the street, customers sitting outside a coffee-house, the mere presence of people whose troubles she didn't know, or who perhaps had none. The mild, warm air around her did her good too, so did the thought that she could experience many such evenings, a thousand such delightful days and nights, and the sense of a healthy *joie de vivre* flowing through her veins. Well, after countless hours of mortal weariness, was she going to feel guilty for coming back to herself, so to speak, just for a minute? Had she no right to relish her own existence? She was healthy, she was young, and from all around, as if from a hundred sources all at once, the joy of being alive flooded over her. It was as natural as her breathing and the sky above her—and is she, she asks herself, to be ashamed of it? She thinks of Felix too. If a miracle happens and he recovers, she will certainly go on living with him. She thinks of him with mild, regretful sorrow. It will soon be time to go back to him. Is he all right only when she is with him? Does he appreciate her loving care? How bitter his words are! How reproachful his glance—and his kiss! It's so long since they kissed each other. She can't help thinking of his lips, always so pale and dry now. She doesn't want to kiss his brow either, it's cold and damp. How ugly illness is!

She leaned back in the cab and deliberately turned her thoughts away from the sick man. And so as not to think of him, she looked eagerly out at the street, observing the scene as closely as if she must imprint it on her memory.

Felix opened his eyes. A candle burning beside his bed gave a faint light. The old maidservant sat beside him, indifferent, her hands in her lap. She jumped when the sick man cried: "Where is she?" The old woman explained that Marie had gone out and would be back very soon.

"You can go!" said Felix. And when the woman hesitated, he repeated, "Go, you can go. I don't need you."

He was alone now, and uneasiness came over him, tormenting him more than ever before.

Where is she, he wondered, where is she? He could hardly bear to wait in bed, but he dared not get up. Suddenly an idea flashed through his mind: perhaps she's gone away and left him! She wants to leave him alone, alone for ever. She can't bear life beside him any more. She's afraid of him, she's read his thoughts. Or he's been talking in his sleep and said out loud what's always lurking in the depths of his consciousness, even if he doesn't give it clear expression for days on end. And she doesn't *want* to die with him.

These ideas chased through his brain. The fever that came every evening was back. It's so long since he has said a kind word to her, he tells himself, perhaps it's just that! He's been tormenting her with his moods, with his suspicious looks, his bitter remarks, when she needed gratitude! Or no, no, merely justice! Oh, if only she were here! He must have her! He admits to himself, with burning pain, that he can't manage without her. He'll apologize to her for everything if need be, he will look at her tenderly again and find words of deep ardour for her. He won't utter a syllable to show how he is suffering. He will smile when he feels heavy at heart. He will kiss her hand when he is struggling for breath. He'll tell her that he dreams nonsensical dreams, and what she hears him say in his sleep is just his fevered imagination. And he will swear that he adores her, that he will let her have a long and happy life, wants her to have it, just so long as she will stay with him to the last, just so long as she doesn't move from his bedside, she mustn't leave him to die alone. He will face that terrible hour in wisdom and calm if only he knows that she is with him! And the hour may come so soon, it may come any day. So she must be with him all the time, for he is afraid when he is without her.

Where is she? Where is she? The blood whirled through his brain, his eyes grew dim, his breath came with more difficulty, and there was no one there. Oh, why had he sent that woman away? She was a human soul, after all. Now he was helpless, helpless. He sat up, feeling stronger than he had thought apart from his difficulty in breathing—that was a terrible torment. He couldn't stand it, he got out of bed and, half-clothed as he was, went to the window. There air—there air ... He took a few deep breaths. How good that was! He picked up the voluminous robe hanging over the end of the bed and dropped into a chair. For a few seconds all his thoughts were in confusion, and then that one question, always the same, kept flashing out. Where is she? Where is she, he asks himself. Has she often left him before like that while he was asleep? Who knows? Where can she be going? Does she just want to escape the stale air of the sickroom for a couple of hours, or is she trying to get away from *him* because he is ill? Does it repel her to be near him? Is she afraid of the shadows of death already hovering here? Does she long for life? Is she looking for life? Doesn't he himself mean life to her any more? What is she seeking? What does she want? Where is she? Where is she?

And his flying thoughts turned to whispered syllables, to words moaned aloud. He screamed, he cried out, "Where is she?" Then he saw her in his mind's eye, perhaps hurrying downstairs, a smile of liberation on her lips, going away, anywhere, to some place without sickness, disgust and slow dying, to some unknown place of fragrance and flowers. He saw her disappear, vanish into a light mist that hid her and from which her rippling laughter sounded, a laugh of happiness and joy. Then the mists parted, and he saw her dancing. She whirled round and round, and disappeared. Now he heard a dull rolling sound coming closer and closer. It suddenly stopped. Where is she? He started with alarm and hurried to the window. It had been the sound of a carriage drawing up outside the building. Yes, certainly, he could see it. And getting out of the carriage—yes, it was Marie! It was Marie! He must go to meet her, he rushed into the next room, but it was completely dark there and he couldn't find the door handle. Then the key turned in the lock, the door flew open and Marie came in, with the faint gas light from the corridor shining around her. Unable to see him in the dark, she collided with him and cried out. He took her shoulders and pulled her into the room. Opening his mouth, he found that he couldn't speak.

"What's the matter?" she cried in horror. "Are you mad?" She drew away from him. He stood there as if rooted to the spot. At last he found words.

"Where have you been—where?"

"For God's sake, Felix, pull yourself together. How could you—! I beg you, do at least sit down."

"Where have you been?" He spoke more quietly this time, as if lost. "Where? Where?" he whispered. She took his hands, which were burning hot. Docile, almost unconscious, he let her lead him to the sofa and slowly press him down into one corner. He looked around as if he had to recover his senses slowly. Then he repeated, distinctly but in the same monotonous manner, "Where have you been?"

She had partly recovered her composure. She threw her hat down on a chair behind her, sat down on the sofa too, and said coaxingly, "Darling, I only went out for an hour in the open air. I was afraid I might fall ill myself, and then what use would I be to you? And I took a cab so as to get back to you quickly."

He was lying in his corner of the sofa, very limp now. He looked askance at her, and did not answer.

She went on, caressing his hot cheeks lovingly. "You're not cross with me, are you? I asked the maid to sit with you until I was back. Didn't you see her? Where is she?"

"I sent her away."

"But why, Felix? She was to wait until I came home. I wanted you so much! What good is the fresh air outside to me if I don't have you?"

"Sweetheart, sweetheart!" Like a sick child, he laid his head on her breast, and as in the old days her lips brushed his hair. Then he looked up at her with pleading eyes. "Sweetheart," he said, "you must stay with me always, always, will you?"

"Yes," she replied, kissing his damp, tangled hair. She felt miserable, unutterably miserable. She would have liked to shed tears, but her emotion had something dry and withered about it. There was no comfort to be found anywhere, even in her own pain. And she envied him, for she saw the tears flowing down his cheeks.

After that she sat at his bedside all through the days and evenings that followed, brought him his meals, gave him medicine, and when he was feeling well enough to ask for it she read aloud to him from the newspaper, or perhaps a chapter from some novel. It had begun to rain the morning after her expedition, and autumn weather came early. Now thin grey rain ran down the windows for hours, days on end, almost without stopping. Recently Marie had heard the invalid talking disjointedly at night. Then she would automatically stroke his forehead and hair, whispering, "Sleep, Felix, sleep, Felix!" as if soothing a restless child. He was becoming visibly weaker, but he did not suffer much, and when the short attacks of breathlessness that reminded him graphically of his illness were over, he usually lapsed into a state of apathy for which he himself could no longer account. But that itself sometimes made him wonder a little: why am I so indifferent to all around me? When he saw the rain falling outside, he told himself: ah yes, autumn, and thought no further about it. Indeed, he could imagine no possible change, neither death nor the recovery of his health. And Marie too could see no prospect of any change at this time. Even Alfred's visits had come to seem habitual. To him, of course, coming from outside, a man for whom life still went on, the sickroom presented a different picture every day. He knew there was no hope. He saw that both Felix and Marie had now entered upon a period that he had sometimes found was experienced by those who had known extreme emotions, a time when there was no hope and no fear, when perception of the present itself was dark and opaque because there could be no looking forward to the future or back to the past. He himself always entered the sickroom with a sense of deep discomfort, and was very glad if he found them both the same as the last time he had left them. For a moment must come when, at last, they would be forced to think of what lay ahead.

On a day when he had climbed the stairs with this thought in his mind again, he found Marie pale-cheeked, standing in the entrance hall and wringing her hands. "Oh, come with me, come with me!" she cried. He followed her quickly. Felix was sitting up in bed. He glared at the two of them as they came in, crying, "What are you really planning for me?"

Alfred went quickly towards him. "What's the matter, Felix?" he asked.

"What are you planning for me? That's what I want to know."

"What sort of childish questions are these?"

"You're both letting me perish, perish miserably!" Felix was almost screaming.

Alfred came close to him and tried to take his hand, but the invalid snatched it back. "Leave me alone, and Marie, you can stop wringing your hands like that. I'd like to know what the two of you are planning. I want to know what's going to happen now."

"Anything that happens," said Alfred calmly, "would go much better if you didn't agitate yourself unnecessarily."

"Listen, how long have I been lying here, how long! You both look at me and then you leave me. What are you planning for me?" he asked the doctor, suddenly turning to him.

"Don't talk nonsense."

"Nothing's going to be done for me, nothing at all. I've only just realised, but you're not going to lift a finger to prevent it!"

"Felix," began Alfred in a firm voice, sitting down on the bed and trying to take his hand again.

"I know what it is, you've given me up for lost. Leaving me just to lie here and take morphine."

"You must be patient for a few more days—"

"But as you can see, it's doing me no good! I can feel the state I'm in. Why do you let me perish without doing anything to save me? You can see I'm going downhill. I can't stop it! And there must be something to be done for it, some kind of help. Think, Alfred, you're a doctor, it's your duty."

"Certainly there's some kind of help," said Alfred.

"Or if not help, perhaps a miracle. But no miracle's going to happen here. I must get out of this place, I want to get out of it."

"As soon as you're strong enough you can leave your bed."

"Alfred, I tell you, it will be too late. Why should I stay in this dreadful room? I want to go away, I want to leave the city. I know what I need. I need spring, I need the south. When the sun shines again I'll be better."

"That all sounds like good sense," said Alfred. "Of course you shall go to the south, but you must have a little patience. You can't travel today, or tomorrow either. You shall go as soon as it's practicable."

"I can travel today, I feel I can. As soon as I'm out of this terrible death chamber I'll be a new man. Every day longer you leave me here is dangerous."

"My dear friend, you must remember that I, as your doctor—"

"As a doctor you think in stereotypes. Sick people know best what they need. It's careless, thoughtless to leave me lying here to rot away. Miracles sometimes do happen in the south. One doesn't fold one's hands in resignation if there's even a little hope, and there *is* still hope. It's inhuman to leave a man to die as you're leaving me. I want to go south. I'll come back in the spring."

"And so you shall," said Alfred.

"We could leave tomorrow, couldn't we?" said Marie, hastily intervening.

"If Felix will just promise to rest for three days, I'll send him away then. But here and now, today—it would be criminal! I can't allow it, not in any circumstances. Just look at the weather," he added, turning to Marie. "It's

wet and windy; I wouldn't advise even the healthiest of
men to travel today."

"Tomorrow, then!"

"If the rain clears up a little," said the Doctor, "then
you can travel in two or three days' time. You have my
word."

The sick man looked at him searchingly. Then he
asked, "Your word of honour?"

"Yes."

"There, do you hear that?" cried Marie.

"You don't believe," said the invalid turning to Alfred,
"there's still any way of saving me? You were going to
let me die in my native land? That's false humanity! A
man on the point of death has no native land any more.
Being able to live at all is his home. And I don't want to
die defenceless, I don't want to."

"My dear Felix, you know very well that I intend you
to spend the whole winter in the south. But I can't let you
travel in weather like this."

"Marie," said the invalid "get everything ready."

She looked at the doctor anxiously, a question in her
eyes.

"Well, it can't hurt," he said.

"Pack everything. I'm going to get up in an hour's time,
and we'll start as soon as the sun comes out again."

Felix got up that afternoon. It was almost as if the
mere idea of a change of scene had a beneficial effect
on him. He was wakeful, and lay on the sofa all the time,
but he had no despairing outbursts, nor did he fall into
the sombre indifference of the last few days. He took an

interest in the preparations that Marie was making, gave directions, told her what books he wanted to take from his library, and himself took from his desk a large sheaf of writings that were to go in the trunk too. "I want to look through some of my old things," he told Marie, and later, as she was trying to cram the documents into the trunk, he returned to the subject. "Who knows, maybe all this resting has done my mind good! I feel positively ready for anything. I sometimes see everything I've ever thought with wonderful clarity."

After the stormy wind and rain, it turned fine again that very day, and the next day was so mild that they could open the windows. Now the light of a warm pleasant autumn afternoon lay over the floor, and when Marie knelt beside the trunk the sun shone in on her waving hair.

Alfred arrived just as Marie was carefully packing the sheaf of papers, while Felix, lying on the sofa, was beginning to discuss these plans of his. "You want me to give permission for that too?" asked Alfred, smiling. "Well, I hope you're going to be careful enough not to start working too soon."

"Oh," said Felix, "it won't be like work for me. I can see new, fresh light thrown on all the ideas that were obscure to me before—thousands of fresh insights."

"Well, that's excellent," said Alfred slowly, as he observed the invalid staring fixedly into space.

"Don't misunderstand me, though," Felix went on. "I have no clearly outlined projects, but I feel as if something were brewing in my mind."

"Good, good."

"It's like hearing the instruments of an orchestra tuning up, you see. That always had a strong effect on me with a real orchestra. And very soon it will play pure harmonies, and all the instruments will join in at just the right places." Then, suddenly getting to his feet, he asked, "Have you booked a compartment on the train?"

"Yes," replied the doctor.

"We'll be off tomorrow morning then," cried Marie cheerfully. She was still busy going from the chest of drawers to the trunk, from the trunk to the bookcase, then back to the trunk, arranging and packing everything. Alfred felt strangely moved. He might have been with a couple of happy young people preparing for a pleasure trip! The mood in the room seemed so full of hope today, almost unclouded. When he left, Marie accompanied him to the door. "Oh, my goodness," she cried "what a good idea it is for us to go away! I'm really looking forward to it. And he's changed so much now that it's real."

Alfred hardly knew what to reply. He shook hands with Marie and turned to go. But then, turning back once more, he told her "You must promise me to—"

"To do what?"

"I mean, I'm more than a doctor, I'm a friend. You know I'm always at your disposal. You need only send me a telegram."

Marie was alarmed. "You think that might be necessary?"

"I mention it just in case." And with these words he left.

She stood there thoughtfully for a while, then quickly returned to the sitting-room, afraid that her brief absence might have upset Felix. But he seemed to have been only waiting for her return to continue with his earlier remarks.

"You know, Marie" he said, "the sun has always done me good. When it gets colder we'll go even further south, to the Riviera, and after that—what do you think of this idea?—to Africa. Yes, I'd be sure to produce a master-piece below the Equator!"

He talked on like this until at last Marie came over to him, stroked his cheeks and said, smiling: "That will do for now. Don't get too reckless all at once. And you ought to go to bed, because we'll have to get up early in the morning." She saw that his cheeks were very flushed and his eyes sparkling, and when she took his hands to help him up from the sofa they were burning hot.

Felix woke at the first light of dawn. He was in the happy, excited mood of a child going on holiday. Two hours before they were to drive to the railway station he was sitting on the sofa, ready to leave. Marie had finished all the packing long before. She wore her grey duster coat and a hat with a blue veil, and was standing thus clad at the window so that she could see the cab they had ordered in good time when it arrived. Felix asked every five minutes if it was there yet. He was getting impatient, and spoke of sending for another when Marie cried, "Here it comes, here it comes. Why," she added next moment, "and here's Alfred too."

Alfred had come around the corner at the same moment as the cab, and was waving cheerfully up to her. Soon he was in the room with them. "Well, I see you two are all ready," he cried. "Why do you want to set off for the station so early? Particularly when, as I see, you've already had breakfast."

"Felix is so impatient," said Marie. Alfred went over to his friend, and the sick man smiled cheerfully at him. "Excellent weather for travelling," he said.

"Yes, it's going to keep fine for you," said the Doctor. He took a rusk from the table. "May I?"

"Goodness, haven't you had breakfast yet?" cried Marie, quite horrified.

"Oh yes, yes. I drank a glass of cognac."

"Wait, there's still some coffee in the pot." She would not be dissuaded from pouring the rest of the coffee into a cup for him, and then went out to give the servant some instructions in the next room. It took Alfred a long time to drink his coffee and put the cup down. He felt awkward alone with his friend, and would not have been able to talk easily. But Marie came back, saying there was nothing to keep them from leaving the apartment now. Felix rose and went out of the door first. He had a grey Inverness cape over his shoulders, wore a soft, dark hat, and carried a walking stick. He intended to be first down the steps outside the building too, but as soon as he touched the balustrade he began to sway. Alfred and Marie, following just behind him, immediately supported him. "I'm a little dizzy," said Felix.

"Only natural" said Alfred, "when you're out of bed

for the first time in several weeks." He took one of the invalid's arms, Marie took the other, and so they led him down the steps. The cab driver took off his hat when he saw the sick man.

Several sympathetic female faces could be seen at the windows of the building opposite. And as Alfred and Marie lifted Felix, who was now as pale as death, into the vehicle, the caretaker too made haste to come up and offer his help. As the cab drove away, he and the sympathetic women exchanged understanding and emotional glances.

Standing on the footboard of the railway carriage, Alfred talked to Marie until the bell rang for the last time. Felix had settled into a corner of their compartment and seemed indifferent to what was going on. Only when the whistle of the engine was heard did he appear to pay attention again, nodding a goodbye to his friend. The train began to move away. Alfred stayed on the platform for a while, watching it, and then slowly turned to go.

As soon as the train was out of the station Marie sat down very close to Felix and asked him what he would like. Should she open the bottle of cognac, would he like her to find him a book, or read aloud to him from the newspaper? He seemed to feel grateful for her kindness, and pressed her hand. Then he asked, "When do we arrive in Merano?" and finally, as she didn't know the precise time of their arrival, asked her to read him all the relevant data from the travel guide. He wanted to know where they would be stopping at midday, where they would be at nightfall, and took an interest in a number of trivial matters to which he was usually entirely indifferent. He tried to work out how many people there might be on the train in all, and wondered if there were any young married couples among them. After a while he said he would like some cognac, but it made him cough so much that he instructed Marie, quite angrily, on no account to give him any more even if he asked for it. Later he got her to read him the weather forecast from the paper, nodding with satisfaction when it proved to be a good one. They were passing through the Semmering region. He looked attentively out of the window at the hills, woods, meadows and mountains, but said nothing except for a quiet, "Pretty, very beautiful," with no pleasure at all in his tone of voice. At midday he ate a little of the cold food they had brought with them, and was angry when Marie refused to give him cognac. In the end she had to let him have some. It went down well this time, he felt better, and began taking an interest in all kinds of things. And soon, in talking about the scenes flying past the windows of their compartment and what he saw in the stations, he returned to the subject of himself. "I've read about somnambulists," he said, "who saw some kind of cure in a dream—something no doctor had thought of, but they tried it and recovered. A sick man should do whatever he wants to do, that's what I say."

"Quite right" replied Marie.

"The south! The air of the south! They say the whole difference is that it's warm there, and there are flowers in bloom all the year round, and perhaps more ozone and no storms and no snow. Who can say what's in the air of the south? Mysterious elements of which we know nothing yet!"

"I'm sure you'll get better there" said Marie, taking one of the sick man's hands between her own and carrying it to her lips.

He talked on, about all the painters to be found in Italy, the fascination of Rome that had attracted so many artists and kings to that city, and Venice, which he had once visited long before he met Marie. At last he felt tired, and decided to lie full length on the seat of the compartment. He stayed there, sleeping lightly most of the time, until evening came.

She sat opposite, looking at him. She felt at peace, and only a little regretful. He was so pale. And he had grown so old. How that handsome face had changed since spring! But it was a different pallor that now lay on her own cheeks. Hers made her look younger, almost virginal. How much better off she was than Felix! The thought had never occurred to her before with such clarity. Why doesn't my pain hurt more, she wondered? Oh, surely not for lack of pity, it's just the boundless weariness that hasn't left her for days, even when she seems to feel better at times. She is glad of her exhaustion, for she fears the pain that will return if she stops feeling tired.

Marie suddenly woke from the sleep into which she had fallen. She looked around her. It was almost dark now. There was a shade over the lamp in the roof of the compartment, so that it cast only a faint, greenish light. And outside the windows it was night! It was as if they were travelling through a long tunnel. Why had she woken with such a violent start? Everything was almost silent but for the constant, monotonous rumble of the wheels. Gradually she accustomed her eyes to the dim light, and now she could make out the sick man's face again. He seemed to be sleeping very peacefully, lying there motionless. Suddenly he sighed, a strange and plaintive sigh. Her heart thudded. He must have moaned like that before, and that was what woke her. But what was this? She looked more closely and saw that he was not asleep. He lay there with his eyes wide open, as she could now see very clearly. She was afraid of those eyes staring into nothing but space and darkness. And she heard another moan, even more plaintive than before. He moved, and now he sighed again, but not painfully, a wild sigh instead. At once he was sitting up, both hands supporting him on the cushions, and then he threw off the grey cape that covered him, kicked it to the floor of the compartment, and tried to stand. But the movement of the train would not let him, and he sank back into the corner of the seat. Marie had jumped up to remove the green shade from the lamp, but she suddenly felt his arms around her, and now he pulled her down on his knees. She was trembling. "Marie, Marie!" he said in a hoarse voice.

She wanted to free herself, but couldn't. All his strength seemed to have returned; he held her powerfully to him. "Are you ready, Marie?" he whispered, with his lips close to her throat. She didn't understand, she merely felt a sensation of boundless fear. She was defenceless and wanted to cry out.

"Are you ready?" he asked again, holding her less convulsively, so that his lips, his breath, his voice were further from her again and she could breathe more easily.

"What do you want?" she asked apprehensively.

"Don't you understand me?" he replied.

"Let go of me, let go of me," she cried, but her voice was lost in the noise of the train rolling on.

He took no notice. Then he let his hands drop, and she rose from his knees and sat down in the corner of the compartment opposite him.

"Don't you understand me?" he asked again.

"What do you want?" she whispered from her own corner.

"I want an answer," he replied.

She said nothing, but trembled, and wished for daylight.

"The hour is coming closer," he said in a lower voice, but leaning forward so that she could catch his words more distinctly. "I am asking if you're ready."

"What hour?"

"Ours! Ours!"

She did understand him now, and her throat felt tight.

"Do you remember, Marie?" he went on, and now there was a mild and almost pleading note in his voice. He took both her hands in his. "You gave me the right to ask," he continued, still in a whisper. "Do you remember?"

She had to some extent composed herself again, for

although the words he spoke were terrible, his eyes had lost that fixed look and his voice its threatening note. He seemed like a humble petitioner. And again he asked, almost querulously, "Do you remember?"

Now she found the strength to reply, although with quivering lips. "Felix, you're being childish."

He didn't seem to hear her. In an even tone, as if something half-forgotten were returning to his mind with new clarity, he said, "It's all coming to an end now, Marie, and we must go, our time is up." There was something spellbinding, resolute, inescapable in those words, softly as they were whispered. For a moment, as he moved closer to her, she felt a terrible fear that he was going to attack and throttle her. She thought of running to the other end of the compartment and breaking the window to call for help, but at that moment he let go of her hands and leaned back as if he had no more to say. Then she found her tongue.

"What nonsense you talk, Felix! And now, when we're going to the south where you'll get better again!" He still leaned back on the seat, apparently lost in thought. She stood up and quickly took the green shade off the lamp. That came as a great relief. It was suddenly light, her heart beat more slowly, and her fears vanished. She sat back in her corner again. He had been looking at the floor, and now raised his eyes to her once more. Then he said slowly, "Marie, morning won't deceive me again. Nor will the south. I know that now."

Marie thought: why does he speak so calmly? Is he trying to lull me into a sense of security? Is he afraid I'll try to save myself? And she resolved to be on her guard. She watched him all the time, hardly listening to his words now and followed all his movements, all his glances.

He said: "Well, you're free. Your promise doesn't bind you. How can I force you? Won't you give me your hand?"

She did, but made sure that her own hand rested above his.

"If only day would come!" he whispered.

"Listen, Felix, listen to what I say" she said now. "You should try to sleep a little. Morning will soon be here, and we'll be in Merano within a few hours."

"I can't sleep any more!" he replied, looking up. At that moment their glances met, and he saw the wary distrust in her eyes. In the same moment it all seemed clear to him. She wanted to make him sleep so that she could get off the train unnoticed at the next station, and run away. "What are you planning?" he cried.

She started nervously. "Nothing."

He tried to get to his feet. As soon as she saw that, she left her corner and fled to the other, far away from him.

"Air!" he cried. "Air!" He opened the window and put his head out into the night air. Marie felt reassured; it was only his shortness of breath that had made him get up so suddenly. She went back to him and gently drew him away from the window. "That can't be good for you," she said. He sank back into his corner, breathing laboriously. She stood in front of him for a while, with one hand on the side of the window opening, and then sat down opposite him again where she had been sitting before. After a while his breathing calmed down, and a soft smile formed on his lips. She looked at him anxiously and in alarm. "I'll close the window," she said.

He nodded. "Morning! Morning!" he cried. Streaks of pink were appearing on the horizon.

After that, they sat facing each other for a long time in silence. At last, with his little smile playing around his mouth again, he said, "You're not ready!"

She was about to say something in her usual manner: that he was being childish, or something of that nature. She couldn't. That smile made any answer impossible.

The train was going more slowly, and in a few minutes' time it reached the station where breakfast was to be served. Waiters ran on around the platform with coffee and rolls. Many of the passengers got out of the train, and there was much noise and shouting. Marie felt as if she had woken from a nightmare. The triviality of all this coming and going on the station did her good. She rose, feeling perfectly safe now, and looked at the platform. After a while she beckoned to a waiter and asked him to hand a cup of coffee in to her. Felix watched as she drank it, but shook his head when she asked whether he would like some.

Soon after that the train moved off again, and as they left the station hall they saw that it was fully light now. And beautiful! The mountains towered up with the red light of early morning pouring over them. Marie determined never to feel afraid of night again. Felix looked out of the window now and then, and seemed to be trying to avoid her eyes. She felt he must be a little ashamed of what had been said last night.

The train stopped several times at short intervals now, and it was a beautiful morning, as warm as summer, when it came into Merano station.

"Here we are!" cried Marie. "At last, at last!"

They had hired a carriage and drove round in search of suitable lodgings. "We don't need to scrimp," said Felix. "My fortune will last long enough." They told the driver to stop at certain villas, and while Felix stayed in the carriage Marie saw round the rooms available to rent and looked at the gardens. They soon found what they wanted, a little house with a small garden. Marie asked the landlady to come out with her to tell the young man sitting in the carriage about the various advantages of the villa, Felix agreed to everything, and a few minutes later the two of them had moved in.

Without really sharing Marie's brisk interest in the house, Felix had withdrawn to the bedroom and was looked briefly around it. It was spacious and comfortable, with pale green wallpaper and a big window that now stood open, so that the whole room was filled with the scent of the garden. The beds were opposite this window, and Felix was so exhausted that he fell full length on one of them.

Meanwhile Marie asked the landlady to show her round, and was particularly pleased with the little garden, which had a tall fence around it. There was a way to get into the garden through a small gate in the far side of the fence, without having to go through the house. Beyond the fence, a broad track led straight to the station, a short cut by comparison with the carriage road which the front of the house faced.

When Marie returned to the room where she had left Felix, she found him lying on the bed. She called out to him, but he did not answer. On coming closer she saw that he was even paler than usual. She called again; no answer, and he didn't move. A terrible fear came over her, and she called to the housekeeper and sent her for a doctor. No sooner had the woman gone than Felix opened his eyes. But just as he was about to say something, he raised himself, his face twisted with fear and he fell back again, breathing stertorously. A little blood was flowing from his lips. Feeling helpless and desperate, Marie bent over him. She went quickly to the door to see if the doctor was coming yet, then hurried back to Felix and called his name. Oh, she thought, if only Alfred were here!

At last the doctor arrived: an elderly man with grey side-whiskers. "Help him, help him!" Marie cried. Then she gave him as much information as she could in her state of agitation. The doctor looked at the sick man, felt his pulse, said he couldn't examine him properly when he had just been bringing up blood, and told her what to do for him. Accompanying the doctor out, Marie asked what she should expect. "I can't say yet," he replied. "Have a little patience, and we'll hope for the best." He promised to come back that evening, and from the carriage he waved to Marie, who was standing in the doorway of the house in as friendly and casual a way as if he had been paying a social call.

Marie stood there at a loss for no more than a second. Next moment she had an idea that seemed to her to promise salvation, and she hurried to the post office to send Alfred a telegram. Once she had dispatched it she felt relieved. She thanked the housekeeper who had been caring for the sick man while she was out, apologized for the inconvenience they had given her on their very first day, and promised that they would show their appreciation.

Felix was still lying unconscious and fully clothed on the bed, but his breath was more regular now. While Marie sat down at the head of the bed the housekeeper comforted her, telling her about all the invalids who had been cured here in Merano and adding that she herself had been in delicate health in her youth and—well, Marie need only look at her!—she had recovered wonderfully well. Even with all the misfortunes she had known. Her husband dead after two years of marriage, her sons now gone out into the world—oh yes, it could all have turned out differently, but now she was glad to have her post looking after this villa. And she couldn't complain of the owner, particularly as he came over from Bolzano only twice a month at the most to see that everything was all right. She rambled on and on, from one subject to the next, brimming over with friendliness. She offered to unpack their baggage, an offer that Marie gratefully accepted, and later brought some lunch to their rooms. There was milk for the invalid, and the slight movements that he was making seemed to suggest that he would soon come round.

At last Felix did return to consciousness, turned his head back and forth several times, and then fixed his gaze on Marie, who was bending over him. He smiled, and pressed her hand faintly. "What happened to me?" he asked.

The doctor, coming later in the day, thought he was much better and said he could be undressed and put to bed. Felix, indifferent, let it all wash over him.

Marie did not move from the sick man's bedside. It was an endless afternoon. The mild scents of the garden came in through the window, which was left open on the doctor's orders—and it was so quiet! Her eyes mechanically followed the movement of the sunlight flickering over the floor. Felix held her hand almost all the time. His own was cool and damp, and Marie did not like the sensation. Sometimes she broke the silence with a few words, and had to force herself to speak them. "You're feeling better, aren't you? ... There, you see! ... No, don't talk ... No, you mustn't ... The day after tomorrow you'll be able to go out in the garden!" And he nodded and smiled. Then Marie tried to work out when Alfred might arrive. He could be here tomorrow evening. Another night and another day, then. Oh, if only he were here!

The afternoon seemed endless. The sun disappeared, the room itself began to lie in twilight, but when Marie looked out into the garden she saw golden sunlight still moving over the white gravel path and the posts of the fence. Suddenly, just as she was looking out of the window, she heard the sick man's voice. "Marie."

She quickly turned her head to him.

"I do feel much better now," he said, in quite a strong voice.

"You mustn't talk too loud," she said lovingly.

"Much better," he whispered. "It turned out all right this time. Perhaps that was the crisis."

"I'm sure it was," she agreed.

"I'm pinning my hopes on the air here. But that mustn't happen again, or I'm done for."

"Hush! You wait and see, you'll soon be feeling better again."

"You're a good girl, Marie, thank you. But look after me well. Take care, take care!"

"Do you have to tell me that?" she asked, in a tone of gentle reproach.

However, he was continuing, in a whisper. "Because if I must go, I'm taking you with me."

Mortal terror flashed through her as he spoke those words. But why? He could be no danger, he was too weak for any act of violence. She was ten times stronger now. What could he be thinking of? What were his eyes seeking in the air, on the wall, in space? He couldn't rise to his feet and stand, and he had no weapons with him. Although poison was possible. He could have bought poison, perhaps he was carrying it with him, and would slip it into her glass. But then where could he be keeping it? She herself had helped to undress him. Maybe he had a powder of some kind in his wallet? But that was in his coat. No, no, no! He had been uttering words inspired by his fever and his wish to torment her, nothing else. But if his fever can inspire such words, such ideas, she thought, then why not the deed itself too? Perhaps he's just planning to use a moment when she's asleep to strangle her. It would take so little force to do that. She could lose consciousness instantly and then be left defenceless. She won't sleep at all tonight, she tells herself—and tomorrow Alfred will be here!

Evening came on, and then night. Felix had not spoken another word, and the smile had disappeared entirely from his lips; he looked straight ahead of him with the same morose gravity. As it grew dark, the housekeeper brought in lighted candles and set about making the bed beside the sick man's. Marie signed to her that it would not be necessary. Felix had noticed. "Why not?" he asked, then immediately adding, "You're too kind, Marie, you ought to get some sleep, I do feel better." She felt as if she heard derision in those words. She did not sleep, but spent the long night that dragged slowly by at his bedside, never once closing her eyes. Felix lay there quietly almost all the time. Now and then she wondered if he might perhaps just be feigning sleep to lull her into a sense of security. She looked more closely, but the uncertain light of the candle mimicked small twitching movements around the invalid's eyes and mouth that confused her. Once she went to the window and looked out into the garden. It was bathed in a soft blue-grey light, and if she leaned a little way out and looked up she could see the moon apparently hovering above the trees. Not a breath of wind was moving, and in the endless silence and still-ness all around it seemed to her as if the posts of the fence, which she could see clearly, were slowly moving forward and then stopping again.

Felix woke after midnight. Marie rearranged his pillows, and in obedience to a sudden impulse took the opportunity of letting her fingers search for anything hidden among them. She still heard his voice in her ears: "If I must go, I'm taking you with me." But would he have said that if he meant it seriously? If he were able to make such a plan at all? Surely he would have been first and foremost intent on keeping it secret. She was being really childish, letting a sick man's disturbed fantasies frighten her. She felt sleepy, and moved her chair away from the bed—just in case. She didn't *want* to go to sleep. but her thoughts began to lose their clarity, and fluttered from the lucid awareness of day into the twilight of grey dreams. Memories rose in her. Memories of days and nights of great happiness. Memories of hours when he had held her in his arms while the breath of the young spring wafted over them and into the room. She had a vague feeling that the fragrance of the garden outside dared not enter here. She had to go to the window again to drink it in, for a sweetish, stale smell seemed to come from the sick man's moist hair, filling the air of the room unpleasantly. What now? If only it were over! Yes, over! She no longer shrank from the idea, and those treacherous words that made hypocritical pity out of the most dreadful wish of all came to her mind. "If only he were at peace!"

And then what? She saw herself sitting on a bench under a tall tree out in the garden, pale and tear-stained. But these signs of grief were only on her face, on the surface. A joyful peace had taken possession of her soul, peace such has she hadn't known for a long, long time. Then she saw the figure that was herself rise, go out into the street, and slowly walk away. For now she could go anywhere she liked.

But amidst all these reveries she remained wakeful enough to listen for the sick man's breathing, which sometimes turned to groans. At last, and hesitantly, morning approached. At first light of dawn the housekeeper appeared in the doorway, and in her kindly manner offered to take over from Marie for the next few hours. Marie accepted with genuine delight. After one last, fleeting glance at Felix, she left the bedroom and went into the room next door, where a sofa was comfortably prepared for her to rest there. Oh, how good that was! She threw herself down on the sofa fully clothed and closed her eyes.

She did not wake up for many hours. A pleasant semi-darkness surrounded her. Narrow shafts of sunlight fell through the cracks in the closed shutters. She quickly rose, and immediately had a clear idea of the situation. Alfred must surely arrive today! That thought helped her to face the sombre atmosphere of the next few hours more bravely. Without hesitation, she went into the next room, and when she opened the door was briefly dazzled by the white cover spread over the sick man's bed. But then she saw the housekeeper, a finger to her lips as she rose from her chair, tiptoeing towards Marie as she entered the room. "He's fast asleep," she whispered, and went on to say that until an hour ago he had been lying awake in a high fever, asking now and then for the young lady. The doctor had come early in the morning, and said the sick man's condition was unchanged. She, the housekeeper, had wanted to wake the young lady at that point, but the doctor himself wouldn't let her, and said he would be back some time in the afternoon.

Marie listened carefully to the good old lady, thanked her for her kindness, and then took her place.

It was a warm, almost sultry day. Midday was approaching. Sunlight and silence lay oppressively over the garden. When Marie looked at the bed, the first thing she saw were the sick man's two thin hands lying on the bedspread, sometimes twitching slightly. His chin had dropped, his face was pale as death, his lips slightly open. His breathing stopped for seconds at a time, and then he began drawing superficial, dragging breaths again. "He'll die before Alfred arrives after all," was the thought that passed through Marie's mind. As Felix lay there, his face had regained an expression of youthful suffering, of relaxation after untold pain, resignation after a hopeless struggle. It was suddenly clear to Marie what had brought such a terrible change to his features recently: the bitterness in them when he looked at *her*. There was surely no hatred in his dreams now, and he was handsome again. She wished he would wake up. Looking at him again, she felt full of unutterable grief and a consuming fear for him. The man she now saw dying was her lover again. In an instant, she realised once more what that meant. All the grief of the inevitable, terrible outcome came over her, and she understood everything again, everything. That he had been her happiness and her life, and she had wanted to die with him, and now the moment was eerily close when all would be over and could never be brought back. And the frozen cold that had come over her heart, the indifference of whole days and nights, merged into a sombre yet indefinable feeling. But now, now, she told herself, it's still all right. He is still alive, breathing, perhaps dreaming. Then, however, he will lie stiff and dead, he'll be buried and lie deep in the ground, in a quiet graveyard over which the monotonous days pass as he moulders away. And she will live, she will live among human beings, while she is aware of the silent grave out there where he rests—he, whom she has loved! Her tears flowed and would not cease. At last she sobbed out loud. Then he moved, and as she quickly passed her handkerchief over her cheeks he opened his eyes and looked at her questioningly for a long time, but said nothing. Then, after a few minutes, he whispered "Come here!". She rose from her chair, bent over him, and he raised his arms as if to put them round her neck. But then he let them drop again, and asked "Have you been crying?"

"No," she quickly replied, putting her hair back from her forehead.

He looked at her long and gravely, and then turned away. He seemed to be thinking.

Marie wondered whether she should tell the sick man about her telegram to Alfred. Ought she to prepare him? No, what would be the point? It would be best for her to act as if she herself were surprised by Alfred's arrival. The whole of the rest of the day passed by in sombre, tense expectation. Outward events passed her by as if in a mist. The doctor's visit was soon over. He found his patient apathetic, only occasionally waking from a fretful half-sleep to ask questions and express wishes, but in a tone of indifference. He asked what the time was, wanted water; the housekeeper went in and out. Marie stayed in the room all the time, usually in the armchair beside the invalid. Now and then she stood at the end of the bed, leaning her arms on it, sometimes she went to the window and looked out at the garden where the shadows of the trees were gradually lengthening, until at last dusk fell over the meadows and paths. It had been a sultry evening, and the light of the candle standing on the bedside table next to the sick man's head scarcely moved. Only when night had fallen, and the moon rose above the grey-blue mountains visible far away in the distance, did a slight wind rise. Marie felt greatly refreshed when it blew over her brow, and it seemed to do the sick man good too. He moved his head and turned his wide eyes to the window. And at last he was breathing deeply.

Marie took his hand, which he had left hanging outside the covers. "Is there anything you want?" she asked.

He slowly withdrew his hand from hers, and said, "Come here, Marie!"

She moved closer, with her head very close to his pillows. He placed his hand on her hair as if in blessing, and let it rest there. Then he said quietly, "Thank you for all your love." She had now laid her head on the pillow next to his, and felt her tears coming again. It was perfectly still in the room. Only the whistle of a railway train sounded in the distance, dying away. Then the stillness of the sultry summer evening returned, heavy, sweet and mysterious. Suddenly Felix sat up in bed, so quickly, so violently that Marie took fright. She raised her head from the pillows and stared into his face. He took Marie's head in both hands as he had often done in moments of wild passion. "Marie" he cried, "I want to remind you now."

"Remind me of what?" she asked, trying to withdraw her head from his hands. But he seemed to have all his strength back, and held it fast.

"Remind you of your promise" he said quickly. "Your promise to die with me." As he spoke these words he had moved very close to her. She felt his breath brush her mouth, and she could not get away. He was speaking, as close to her as if she were to drink in his words with her own lips. "I'm taking you with me, I don't want to go alone. I love you, I'm not leaving you here!"

Fear seemed to paralyse her. A hoarse scream broke from her throat, but in a stifled tone so that she could hardly hear it herself. Her head was immovable between his hands, which were convulsively pressing her temples and cheeks. He was still speaking, and his hot, moist breath burned close to her.

"Together! Together! That was what you wanted. And I'm afraid to die alone. Will you come with me? Will you?"

She had pushed away the chair from under her with her feet, and at last, as if freeing herself from an iron clamp, she wrenched her head out of the clutch of his two hands. He kept those hands in the air as if her head were still between them and stared at her as if unable to grasp what was happening.

"No, no!" she cried. "I don't want to!" And she ran to the door. He raised himself to jump out of the bed, but now his strength left him, and he sank back on it with a dull impact, like a lifeless mass. But she wasn't looking at him any more; she had flung the door open and was running through the next room and into the passage. She wasn't in control of herself. He had been going to strangle her! She still felt his fingers sliding down her temples, her cheeks, her throat. She ran out of the house. There was no one outside the door, and she remembered that the housekeeper had gone out to get something for supper. What should she do? She ran back again, along the corridor, into the garden. As if she were being pursued she hastily went across the grass and to the other end of the path. Now she turned, and could see the open window of the room which she had just left. She saw the candlelight flickering there, but that was all. She didn't know what to do. Aimlessly, she walked up and down the path by the garden fence. Now an idea shot through her head. Alfred! He'll be coming now, she thought! He must come now! She looked through the bars of the fence to the moon-lit path leading from the station, hurried to the garden gate, and opened it. There lay the path before her, white and deserted. But perhaps he'll be coming the other way, along the street, she told herself. No, no—there, she sees a shadow approaching, closer and closer, faster, ever fast, the figure of a man. Is it his? She hurried a few steps towards him. "Alfred!"

"Is that you, Marie?"

It was Alfred. She could have wept for joy. When he was beside her she felt like kissing his hand.

"What's the matter?" he asked.

She drew him along with her, without replying.

Felix had lain motionless only for a moment. Then he raised himself and looked around. She had gone, he was alone! Fear came over him, constricting his throat. Only one thing was clear to him: he must have her there, there with him. With one bound he was out of the bed. But he couldn't stand upright, and fell back on it again. He felt a humming and echoing in his head. Supporting himself on the chair, pushing it ahead of him, he moved forward. "Marie, Marie!" he murmured. "I don't want to die alone, I can't!" Where was she? Where could she be? Still pushing the chair, he had reached the window. There lay the garden, and over it the blue radiance of the hot night. How it swirled and shimmered! How the grass and trees danced! Ah, this was spring, and it would make him well again! This air, this air! If such air always blew around him he was sure to get better. There—what was that? And he saw a female figure coming down the shining white path leading from the bars of the fence, which seemed to lie deep in an abyss. The blue moonlight played around her. How she floated, how she flew, yet she came no closer! Marie! Marie! And a man right behind her. A man with Marie—immensely tall. Now the bars of the fence began to dance, danced after the two of them, and so did the dark sky, and everything, everything was dancing after them. And music and sound and singing came from far away, so beautiful, so beautiful. Then all turned dark.

Marie and Alfred arrived, both of them running. When she reached the window Marie stopped and looked anxiously into the bedroom. "He isn't there!" she cried. "The bed's empty!" Suddenly she screamed, and fell back into Alfred's arms. He gently put her aside and leaned over the sill, and then, right beside the window, he saw his friend lying on the floor in his white shirt, full length, his legs spread apart, and beside him an overturned chair. He was holding its back with one hand. A trickle of blood was running down his chin. His lips seemed to move, and so did his eyelids, but when Alfred looked more closely he saw that it was only the moonlight, playing deceptively over that pale face.

ARTHUR SCHNITZLER

Fräulein Else

Translated from the German by F H Lyon

Fräulein Else is the story of a young woman who, while staying with her aunt at a fashionable spa, receives a telegram from her mother begging her to save her father from debtor's jail by approaching an elderly acquaintance in order to borrow money from him. Else is forced into the reality of a world entirely at odds with her romantic imagination, with horrific consequences.

Arthur Schnitzler was born in Vienna in 1862, the son of a prominent Jewish doctor, and studied medicine at the University of Vienna. In later years he devoted his time to writing and was successful as a novelist, dramatist and short-story writer. Schnitzler's work shows a remarkable ability to create atmosphere and a profound understanding of human motives.

ISBN 1 901285 06 5 • *112 pages* • *£6.99*

ANTAL SZERB

Journey by Moonlight

Translated from the Hungarian by Len Rix

Anxious to please his bourgeois father, Mihály has joined the family firm in Budapest. Pursued by nostalgia for his bohemian youth, he seeks escape in marriage to Erzsi. On their honeymoon in Italy, Mihály 'loses' his bride at a provincial station and embarks on a chaotic and bizarre journey that leads him finally to Rome. There all the death-haunted and erotic elements of his past converge, and he, like Erzsi, has finally to choose.

Antal Szerb was born in 1901 into a cultivated Budapest family of Jewish descent. He rapidly established himself as a prolific scholar, publishing books on drama and poetry. His first novel, *The Pendragon Legend*, also published by Pushkin Press, appeared in 1937. He died in the forced-labour camp at Balf in 1945

ISBN 1 901285 50 2 • *240 pages* • £6.99

STEFAN ZWEIG

Amok and Other Stories

Translated from the German by Anthea Bell

A doctor in the Dutch East Indies torn between his medical duty to help and his own mixed emotions; a middle-aged maidservant whose devotion to her master leads her to commit a terrible act; a hotel waiter whose love for an unapproachable aristocratic beauty culminates in an almost lyrical death and a prisoner-of-war longing to be home again in Russia.

In these four stories, Stefan Zweig shows his gift for the acute analysis of emotional dilemmas.

Stefan Zweig was born in 1881 in Vienna, a member of an Austrian-Jewish family. Zweig travelled widely, living in Salzburg between the wars, and enjoying literary fame. In 1934, with the rise of Nazism, he briefly moved to London, finally settling in Brazil, where in 1942 he and his wife were found dead in an apparent double suicide.

ISBN 1 901285 66 9 • *144 pages* • *£7.99*